3 8002 02258 339 9
D1685370

COVENTRY LIBR/

Pl-

PAS-DE-DEUX

Turner Gideon

Gretton Books
Cambridge

First published in 2016 by Gretton Books

© Turner Gideon 2016

The moral right of Turner Gideon to be identified as the author of this work has been asserted in accordance with the Copyright, Design and Patents Act 1988

All rights reserved. Apart from any use permitted under UK copyright law no part of this publication may be reproduced, stored in a retrieval system, or transmitted, in any form or by any means without the prior written permission of the publisher, nor be otherwise circulated in any form of binding or cover other than that in which it is published and without a similar condition being imposed on the subsequent purchaser.

A CIP catalogue record for this title is available from the British Library.

ISBN 978-0-9562041-6-5

Set in 9/11 pt Calibri

Printed and bound by 4edge in the UK

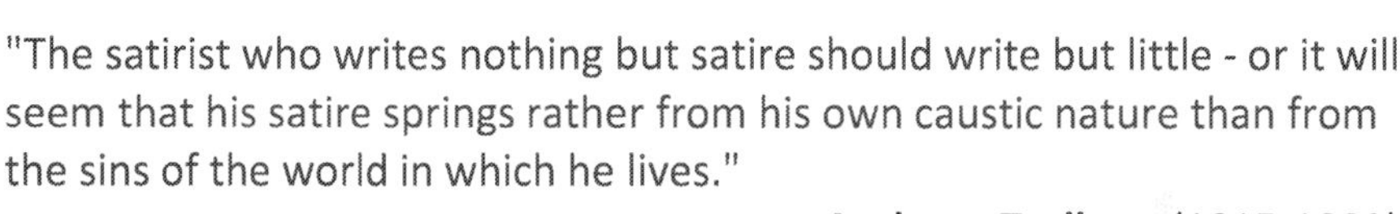

"The satirist who writes nothing but satire should write but little - or it will seem that his satire springs rather from his own caustic nature than from the sins of the world in which he lives."

Anthony Trollope (1815-1882)

"I had a sense he was offering things abominable to me, like decaffeinated coffee or *coitus interruptus*."

Muriel Spark (1918-2006)

This is a work of fiction and any resemblance to people or places living or dead is purely coincidental.

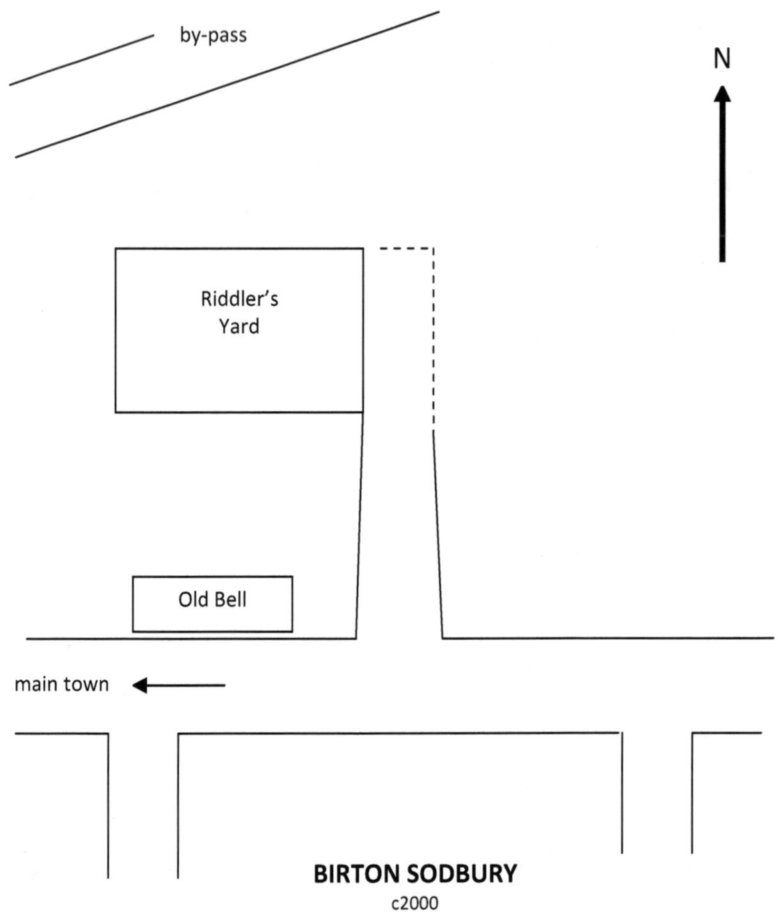

BIRTON SODBURY

c2000

1

"Brilliantly conceived, beautifully executed."

"A bunch of no-hopers aspiring to be less than useless."

Similar views were probably being expressed at that very moment in hundreds of pubs across the country. Not the same conversations of course, and certainly not the same topic, but equally opposed positions being taken. Strong drink, strong emotions and passionate views, not necessarily passionately held. Often just about passing the time. What irritated Hacker was that he had heard these sentiments expressed a hundred times over the last few months. He had no illusions that the strength of the comments reflected the seriousness of the topic. It was bad enough that the conversation was not about war, or politics, or even art (when had he heard that last discussed?); nor thankfully was it about football. Yet again it was about angling permits. He had decided some time ago not to take a stand, not on the question itself. He had a view, and he could understand why many thought an injustice had been perpetrated, why people felt so strongly about the topic and why they kept coming back to it. He could also understand the attractions of fishing, the quiet and solitude, the opportunity to contemplate - or the opportunity not to. Some other landlords might have decided that it was not a good business strategy to express a view. Hacker hoped he was above that. It was simply that there were only so many times he was prepared to go round the same conversational loop. Hacker went through to the other bar and started setting up for the evening.

He was still getting things ready when the door clicked open. It was very unusual for anyone to come in to the lounge at eight on a Tuesday, even more unusual for it to be a woman and, when she closed the door behind her, especially a woman on her own. She was wearing faded jeans and a long pullover. Her black hair streamed over her shoulders. She looked around the room and came up to the bar. Hacker got to his feet.

"Evening," he said. "Can I help you?" He assumed she had come in to ask directions.

"Yes, I'll have a double vodka and tonic, thanks."

"Sure. Ice and lemon?"

"Just ice thanks."

She sat down on one of the stools at the bar and took a long look round. "Quiet," she said, as he handed her the drink.

"Yes, it always is at this time – especially on a Tuesday."

She handed over the money.

"You're not from round here, are you?" he asked.

"No, I'm not. Or not yet anyway."

"How do you mean?"

"I'm thinking of buying the farmhouse."

"What – Riddler's Yard?" Hacker was taken aback. "It's virtually derelict."

"It is now," she said. "But I can see the possibilities – and the location is excellent."

"It'll take a hell of a lot to turn that into a home – a hell of a lot of time and even more money," Hacker said.

"It's been on the market for a while then, I take it?"

"At least a couple of years – no, it's probably nearer three since Mrs Riddler died. Her family have been trying to sell it ever since."

"Couldn't they sell it with the land?"

"No, the land was sold before when her husband died. That was over ten years ago - before I came here."

"And when was that?"

"Getting on for eight years now."

She took some nuts from the bowl on the bar. "You must like it to have stayed that long?"

"Yes, I suppose I must." Hacker paused. "Look, you'll have to excuse me for a moment. There are some things I have to do out the back. Give me a shout if you want anything."

Hacker took the last couple of bottles from the crate he'd been emptying when she came in and stacked them on the cold shelf. He picked up the empty crate and took it out through the kitchen to the store at the back. He locked the store and hung the key back on the peg in the kitchen. Then he got a jar of olives from the fridge and a couple of lemons. He sliced the lemons, discarded the ends and put the slices into a bowl. He washed and dried his hands, and went over to the window ledge where he kept his cigarettes and matches. He opened the back door and stepped outside. A few years ago he would have gone back into the bar and had a cigarette there, but not now. He might have an occasional one after hours in the bar, but he usually smoked outside these days. He supposed it was more professional, and more hygienic, not to smoke behind the bar, but it felt like yet another way in which the moral majority and the health faddists were pressing down on choice, reducing personal freedom. Soon the customers would have no option but to smoke outside too.

Hacker's eyes followed the trail of smoke as it curled off into the night. Apart from the lock-up store and the washing line, the back yard was empty. A row of leylandii marked the boundary between his yard and the fields that began just beyond them. At one end of the leylandii was his garage, separating the yard from the car park, and on the other a wooden fence running from the back wall of the pub down to the trees. As Hacker looked towards the fence, his eyes were drawn to the roof of Riddler's Yard in the distance. Why on earth would a young woman want to take that on? She didn't look like she was into DIY. Nor had she said "We're", but "I'm" thinking of buying it. Yet she looked more like someone who would be at home in the city, rather than in a town or a small village like this. He stubbed out the cigarette in the sand-bucket and went back into the kitchen. He took the olives and bowl of lemon through to the bar. She was standing on the other side of the room looking at the collection of photographs of village life going back over the last hundred years. They were a fairly bog-standard set, Hacker thought, but as they'd been there when he had taken over the pub and he didn't have anything better to replace them with, he'd left them up. They provided some interest for passing trade from time to time, though there was considerably less of this since the by-pass had opened.

"Have you been round the farmhouse yet?" Hacker asked.

"Yes, I went round with the agent this afternoon. In fact I liked it so much I've made an offer. I'm hoping to hear in the next day or two."

"Well, if we're going to be neighbours, I'd better introduce myself. I'm Hacker ... Hacker Black."

Hacker could barely remember being called anything else. It hadn't been his original name, but even his parents had realised early on that Christian had not been the most appropriate choice. Abbreviating it to Chris seemed even less appropriate somehow. Once all his friends at school started calling him Hacker, his parents eventually succumbed and used it too. Even Hacker was no longer sure how it had started off or why: perhaps it had something to do with his efforts at sport, but whether on the football or rugby fields, or his less successful efforts on the golf course, he wasn't sure. No matter how it had started, and some of his friends had much more scurrilous explanations which he had usually been happy to encourage, it suited him admirably. Over six feet tall, burly but not fat, with black eyes and hair, it could have been made for him.

Hacker came round the end of the bar into the lounge area. "And what's your's?" he asked as he reached out to shake her hand.

"Euphony," she said, and drank the remains of her vodka. When she took his hand, her grip was as firm as his. Hacker could feel her certainty and determination, in this and in the way she looked directly into his eyes.

"That's an unusual name," Hacker said. "Even more unusual than mine. But your's sounds much better."

Euphony laughed. "That's also what it means of course."

"Sorry? Oh yes, of course, I see," said Hacker. "There can't be many people with that name. Unique I should think."

"I've certainly never come across one," Euphony said. "That's probably what my mother intended. She was always determined that I should stand out." She paused. "I'd better be going. I've got a long drive back."

"Well, nice to meet you," Hacker said. "Best of luck with the farmhouse." Strangely enough he meant it.

"Thanks," she said. She went to the door. As she opened it, she turned back towards Hacker. "I'm sure we'll meet again. By the way, my second name is Blurr. Bye." She went out.

"Bye," said Hacker, more to himself than her as the door closed behind her.

He went back towards the bar. "Euphony Blurr," he thought to himself, "now that is a name to conjure with". Despite its improbability, it never occurred to him that it might not be real. Her manner made it apparent she didn't play games like that, or, if she did, was so good at it that you were none the wiser anyway. Leaning over the bar he took a pound from the till and went to put it in the jukebox. The music began playing. As if on cue the door opened again.

"Evening, Tom," said Hacker.

"Evening," said the man.

"Usual?"

The man nodded as he shut the door behind him. He came over and sat at the table by the bar, in the seat he always occupied. His Jack Russell settled at his feet.

"Good day?" asked Hacker as he passed Tom his pint.

"Not so bad," said Tom, "though my leg's been better. Who was that?"

"Someone who's been looking at the Riddlers' place."

"Must have more money than sense if they buy that."

Hacker's evening started up.

2

Hacker's pub, The Old Bell, was moderately successful, and Hacker was good at running it. Over the years he had developed a mixture of warmth and firmness that conveyed itself to his customers. They had found they liked it, and knowing where they stood when they came there, they kept coming because of the comfort and certainty it afforded them. Hacker had bought the pub cheaply from the previous landlord who had left after only a few months. This man had not endeared himself to the village through his marketing efforts, which included karaoke nights and a sign on the pavement saying 'It's nice to be important, but more important to be nice'. This was so at odds with his personal style, which was anything but nice, that he was treated with contempt. He had also attracted a group of cronies from the nearby town who drank there till all hours and drew the attentions of the police. His tenure ended in a blaze of publicity when a raid in the early hours uncovered drugs and under-age drinking. He was not in a position to demand a high price.

It had taken Hacker almost a year to recover the pub's reputation with the village. After their previous experience, the villagers kept a close eye on him in the early months to see how he did. There was little chance of the anonymity that had attracted him to Birton Sodbury in the first place. He realised very rapidly that he had made a mistake in this respect. Birton Sodbury might well be unknown to the surrounding world, but the same was not going to be allowed to apply to him unless he worked at it. He suspected that the 'Old Sods', as the long-standing residents described themselves, had been instrumental in alerting the police to the previous landlord's activities. They weren't quite a vigilante group, but they were vigilant in guarding what they saw as proper standards of Birton life. By 'proper' they meant 'as before', or more fully 'if this wasn't as it was before, it should have been'. He was sure they wouldn't hesitate to act again if they felt he wasn't keeping up to the mark.

As it happened, Hacker's desire for a quiet life coincided with their view of what was proper for the village pub. Although he had never done anything like this before, Hacker found that he enjoyed being a pub-keeper. While the grinding routine and the long hours wore him down sometimes, it had several compensations. It provided him with a reasonable living and he was his own boss. He got on well with the mix of regulars. They brought with them a degree of friendship, or at least companionship, but also maintained a distance that Hacker found re-assuring. It suited Hacker that, while there was a fair amount of predictability from one day to the next, occasionally the unexpected and the unusual could take place – but generally within tolerable bounds. He felt in control of the situation, but without having to exert himself unduly to achieve it. In other words, he was coasting.

This had not always been the case.

3

When Hacker had left school almost thirty years previously, he had been unclear what to do next. There was no tradition in his family of higher education, and, even if there had been, his results were not good enough. While he was thinking through his options, he spent the summer working for an import company on the outskirts of Oldham, his home town.

Big Jim's warehouse was essentially a collection of sheds at the end of a long lane. Big Jim shipped in novelty goods from abroad, eastern Europe mainly, held them for as little time as possible and then sold them on to the shops, fairs and other outlets around the country that had a market for something a bit different, but not very well made and consequently cheap. Big Jim did all the ordering and most of the delivering himself, his wife kept the books and his two sons looked after the warehouse, doing the unloading of the lorries and the loading of Big Jim's delivery van. It was therefore a tight-knit family business which, given all the scams Big Jim was involved in, was the way he would have preferred to keep it. However, he had little alternative but to take on an extra pair of hands when his younger son managed to unload a pallet on to his brother, breaking his right arm and both his legs. This may not have been an accident as they had never got on very well, but it was certainly going to prevent the older brother from doing any heavy lifting for the foreseeable future. It was also going to inhibit his developing relationship with a young woman called Maisie, who was almost as well-known around the town as was Big Jim himself. This gave the younger brother an opportunity to cultivate Maisie's acquaintance himself, though needless to say he had to do so covertly. As far as was known, this was a possibility that had not occurred to him before the 'accident'.

Hacker therefore joined Big Jim's at a time when it was under pressure if not quite in danger of falling apart.

"Ever done anything like this before?", Big Jim asked him.

"No."

"It shouldn't be a problem for a big lad like you. It's mostly following the instructions my wife'll give you. So, if you do as you're told, you'll be OK. I'll give you a try for the rest of the week at ten bob an hour. How's that sound?"

"OK," said Hacker. "When do I start?"

"Now, if you can. We could do with some help."

At first Hacker viewed the job as entirely physical. Either he unloaded the new arrivals into whatever space was available, or he followed the instructions on his pick-list for the next day's delivery. Apart from the odd bit of sweeping and tidying that was all there was to it.

But he soon realised that his physical contribution to the process depended entirely on the ability of Big Jim's wife to recall what had gone where. His pick-list detailed not only which row and rack to go to in each shed for each item, but where he'd find each box within that rack. This was effectively an inventory system that operated with computerised efficiency long before computers that could have coped with the task were available – or if they had been would have taken up as much space as the stock.

"How does your mother do this?", he asked Arnold her younger son early in his second week. "How does she remember where everything is?"

"Dunno," said Arnold. "Habit I expect."

"No, it's more than that. She must have some system."

"Could be. Never thought about it myself."

Hacker was not surprised, since it had occurred to him within hours of starting at Big Jim's that thinking was not something Arnold was keen on. He seemed to pursue his life on a simple cause and effect basis: he did what he did either 'cause he wanted to or 'cause he had to.

Big Jim's wife appeared to be as taciturn as her son. Apart from giving Hacker his instructions each day and his money at the end of the week, she said little to him. He didn't even know her name. He thought he'd wait a day or two to see if he could work her system out for himself. If not, he'd have to ask her.

But the following day she came up to him while he was eating his lunch.

"Have you worked it out then?"

"Sorry?", Hacker replied.

"My system. Have you worked out my system for keeping track of all this stuff?"

"No, not yet. Arnold told you then?"

"Arnold never tells me anything. I could see you were trying to puzzle it out."

Hacker didn't know whether to believe this, but perhaps she was as good at intuition as she was at stock control.

"Do you want me to tell you then, or do you want to work it out for yourself?"

"You'd better tell me. Put me out of my misery," Hacker said.

"First thing you have to realise is that when we came here the sheds were totally unuseable. They were damp, and anything stored overnight in the winter would soon rot. Jim and I did them all up ourselves – mended the roofs, laid new floors off the ground, just the two of us. This was not long after the war and I came to think of the sheds as the countries liberated in Europe. From the gate it goes France, Belgium, Holland and so on. Then, when the goods come in, I remember where they've gone in each shed by associating them with the geography of that country. So the rows in France are Normandy, Brittany, Loire, Alps. The racks are towns on the top deck and rivers on the bottom one. I can actually see each item sitting in the town or floating on the river. So all I have to remember is which item is in which town or on which river. All the rest follows."

Hacker didn't know what to say. She made it all sound so matter of fact, but it was clearly a huge feat of memory.

"But don't you get confused between the sheds and where things come from?", he asked.

"No, most of our stuff comes from places like Yugoslavia, Poland, Greece and a little from North Africa. The sheds stop at Italy, so I don't often get it wrong."

"But you still must have a fantastic memory."

"No better than most I expect. It's a case of having to. If I didn't do it, the business would be in a hell of a mess."

"Well, I'm still impressed. I wouldn't be able to come up with five towns for each country, let alone each region – and rivers I wouldn't have a clue about."

"Nor did I at your age. But my dad and both his brothers were in the army. Following the war across Europe introduced me to a whole lot of places I'd never heard of before. And in circumstances that meant I wasn't likely to forget them either."

Not knowing how to respond to this, and not wanting to show this by just staring at her, Hacker said lamely, "Thank God for the war then".

"But you're missing the point," she said quickly. "The point is not what my system is. It could be anything; this one just happens to make sense to me. The point is that I have a system. And I have a system because I have to have a system. It would all fall apart otherwise. Think about it."

With that, she walked off as abruptly as she had arrived.

Although Hacker was only dimly aware of it, he somehow felt he had learned something more useful than anything he'd been taught at school. But whether this was about being in control of your situation, or the flexibility of the human mind in adversity, or its capacity, or just about the benefits of being systematic, he wasn't sure. Probably it was all of them; or then again perhaps it was mainly about men's dependence, even reliance, on women to create order out of chaos. Was it all men, some men, most men? What Hacker was sure about was that he would have to think about it if he was going to get it straight in his head.

One of the immediate consequences of this conversation was that it engendered huge respect in Hacker for Big Jim's wife. To a certain extent this also led him to upgrade his opinions of Big Jim and Arnold as well on the basis of their association with her. While they didn't have her spark of ingenuity, Big Jim did know what would sell, and both he and Arnold were prepared to put in the hard physical effort that was required to keep the momentum of the business going.

As the weeks went by, it became apparent that Hacker had also earned their appreciation. "You're doing all right, son," Big Jim said to him one day. This was high praise, Hacker realised. Even Arnold became more open and talkative, though he and Hacker never gelled fully despite their similar ages.

The weeks Hacker had expected to spend there turned into months but, as October set in and their seasonal outlets began to close down, things were no longer so busy. Big Jim was not out every day on the deliveries as he had been before and there was less for Hacker to do. Rather than wait for Big Jim to raise the subject, Hacker broached it himself.

"You don't really need me any more, do you?", he said to Big Jim when he handed across his week's wages.

"Not really, son," Big Jim replied. "Gone a bit quiet, hasn't it? But," he added, "we could still do with a bit of help for a week or two you know."

"That's OK," Hacker said, "it's time I moved on anyway. My mum and dad are always on at me to get something regular."

"Do you know what?", Big Jim asked.

"I've got a few ideas," Hacker said.

"Right, if you need a word putting in, let me know. I'd be more than happy, and I'm well known round here you know."

"Thanks," Hacker said.

So, at the end of that day Hacker said his farewells. Big Jim and his wife, and Arnold, waved him off and Hacker walked away down the lane for the last time. He fingered the extra fiver that Big Jim had pressed on him when they had shaken hands. "Have a drink on us," he had said. "You've earned it."

Hacker turned at the bend in the lane to give a final wave, but they had already gone back into the sheds to lock up for the weekend. Some people would have been upset by this, but Hacker knew not to take it personally. Actually, he appreciated their open lack of sentiment. It had been a straightforward business transaction, with benefits on both sides. There was no need to pretend that it was something more meaningful. And, in any case, Hacker had got a lot out of it. He now knew what he wanted to do next.

4

The conversation with Big Jim's wife had started Hacker thinking about the power of information when it is systematised. Not just an addition to memory but a spur to action too. This realisation had come together with the conversations he and his friends had each week about what they were going to do on Friday and Saturday nights. It was easy enough to choose between the options in Oldham: there were two discos and three other venues where you could go to see rock bands. But only one of these was on the national tour circuit; the other two were pubs, so only attracted local groups who were still trying to make it. And that essentially was it. The alternatives were to go to somebody's house, find a party or stay in the local. Worse still you could stay in and watch Match of the Day and Parkinson with the family.

A similar set of choices was available in a number of other towns in the area, but even though many of them were only a short bus ride away, they might as well have been a foreign country for all the knowledge that Hacker and his friends had of them. Manchester itself of course had considerably more to offer, and from time to time they did go there. But often they found out about something they would have liked to go to after it had happened rather than before.

Hacker knew that it was not he and his friends that were unusual in this respect. There simply was not the information available in advance that would let people choose ahead. Yet his generation often had the cash in their pockets that would allow them to make such choices. They were not content to stick with the limited range that their parents had been accustomed to and had no alternative but to accept.

Occasionally, they would decide at the start of the week that they would find out what was going on in Manchester the following Saturday. But putting this into practice was tortuous. Only one of Hacker's friends had a phone at home and his parents weren't prepared for it to be used as a public facility. They couldn't afford it any more than Hacker's parents could have done. So it meant queuing up to use phone boxes, hoping to get through before the rest of the queue started banging on the window, and hitting on something early enough in the week to be able to get there in time to book a place. They rarely managed to pull it off.

When they did get to Manchester or one of the other towns it had either been to a disco or, once or twice, to a concert that had been trailed well in advance in *New Musical Express* or *Sounds*.

Hacker decided to do something about this, not as a business opportunity, or not initially at any rate, but as an activity that would meet his needs, those of his friends and many other similar young people in the greater Manchester area. He viewed it more as a service than as a way of making money.

So, on the following Monday, Hacker headed into the centre of Oldham. He went first to the Exchange, the hall that did feature in some bands' tours around the country. They had a poster outside advertising the concerts that were on over the next two weeks. Since he doubted he would get anything out before the end of the week, he took a note only of those that were on in the following week. He was just completing the list when a man went past him up the steps, unlocked the door and went in.

"Excuse me," Hacker said before the man shut the door.

"We open at 10.30," the man said. "You can buy tickets then."

"I don't want any tickets – or not yet. I want to see the manager."

The man looked Hacker up and down. "Do you have an appointment?"

"No, but I've got an idea he might be interested in."

"What sort of idea?"

"Something that could help sell tickets," Hacker said.

"We've got plenty of ideas for selling tickets. In fact, selling tickets is the least of our problems."

"I bet some of your tickets sell themselves," Hacker said. "But I also bet not all of them do."

"Most of our concerts are pretty full."

"What if I said I could help get them all full?"

The man looked him up and down again, but with more interest this time. "Oh, come in then. But this had better be good. I haven't got time to waste – especially not on a Monday morning."

"You won't be disappointed," Hacker promised.

The man let Hacker into the building and led him into an office just off the foyer.

"Are you the manager then?", Hacker asked.

"Good as," said the man, but without explaining what he meant by this. "So, what's this bright idea of your's then?"

Hacker knew he would only have the one chance to get his proposal across. He would have to get it right. This helped crystallise his thoughts. He explained the difficulties he and his friends had in finding out what was happening throughout the area and how he planned to rectify this. In a burst of inspiration he said, "I'm starting a monthly listing called 'Who's Where When'. It'll cover all the music venues in the greater

Manchester area and set out times and prices, phone numbers for bookings, and so on. What do you think of that then?"

The man had been watching Hacker closely as he spoke and didn't reply immediately to the question.

"Well, what do you think? Good or what?", Hacker asked again. "Course what I need is to know what's on here for the rest of the month."

"Look, I don't want to disappoint you, but I don't think it will work," the man said.

"Why not?" Hacker was crestfallen.

"I can see three problems for a start. First, do you have any idea how many places in the Manchester area have live events? Over 100, at least. Not all of them will have something on every night, but even if on average they have three a week, that's 1200 you'll have to list each month. That means that it's going to be a very long listing. Which means, and here's the second problem, it's going to need proper printing equipment. Even then it's going to take time and it's going to cost. And then the third problem is how you're going to sell it at a reasonable price. Oh yes, and I've thought of a fourth: how are you going to distribute it?"

Hacker was taken aback. He could see these were genuine problems that he hadn't thought about. At least the man was not patronising him.

"And there is another problem as well, of course."

"Yes?"

"Some places won't welcome it at all. Not everybody likes competition. Some will think it'll reduce their audience rather than increase it. You and your friends may get more choice, but some places rely on their customers not having much choice. They wouldn't survive if they did."

This was another point that Hacker had not thought about. He had only considered the idea from the viewpoint of himself and his friends. He hadn't considered at all what some venues might make of it.

"But if it means more people go overall, then everybody's likely to benefit – including most of the venues," Hacker said.

"Perhaps. But only if you can get it out to enough people. And that brings us back to the distribution and price problems."

Hacker got up from his chair. "OK. You obviously don't think it's a starter. But you've given me some things to think about, so I appreciate that. It would help if you could tell me what's on here for the rest of the month though, so I don't have to come back again – not till next month anyway."

The man smiled. "So, you're not put off then?"

"Yes, I am put off," Hacker said. "But that doesn't mean I'm going to give up on it just like that."

The man smiled again. "Look, sit down. I didn't say it couldn't be made to work. In fact, I'm pretty sure it can. All I meant was that I didn't think it could work in quite the way you explained it. What's your name by the way? I'm Mac, Neil McKnock really, but everyone calls me Mac." He reached across his desk to grasp Hacker's hand."

Hacker introduced himself and then sat down again.

"Fancy a cup of tea?", Mac asked.

Hacker nodded.

While Mac went out to make the tea, Hacker looked round at the office. On one wall there were high windows at head height with frosted glass. Behind the desk was a large bookcase with manila files lying on their sides in piles. In the corner next to the bookcase were cardboard boxes on top of each other. Opposite the windows some framed playbills advertising plays Hacker had never heard of. Hacker was just turning round to look at the rest of the room when Mac came back in.

"Here you are," Mac said, handing Hacker a cup of tea. Mac went round behind the desk again and leant back in his chair.

"How many of you are working on this, Hacker?", he asked.

"Only me," Hacker said.

"So how were you planning to get it printed and distributed?"

"I hadn't sorted that out yet. I suppose I was hoping to get it run off somewhere and then take it round schools, pubs, shops."

"It'll take you months to do that on your own."

"Yes, I realise that now," Hacker said flatly. "What do you suggest?"

"Cutting it down to a weekly would reduce the cost of printing it and make it more saleable."

"Yes, but it would also mean going round more often to find out what's on. And the speed of distribution would be even more critical," Hacker said.

"You could still collect the information on a monthly basis, but just use it each week. And, if it works, people will soon be coming to you to give you the information so you won't have to go round at all."

"And the distribution?"

"You need to piggy-back on an existing distribution network. Tying it to a local paper might also help on the printing side."

"Yes, but then it just becomes their operation rather than mine," Hacker said.

"Not necessarily," Mac said. "You could maintain the control and pay them to distribute it, or you could even add it as an insert to the paper and agree a slice of the extra copies sold as your share."

"This is way over my head," Hacker said. "I was only aiming to print a couple of thousand copies initially. I don't have the money to start with the sort of operation you're talking about."

"You wouldn't necessarily need any money up-front at all. I know one or two people who would be prepared to give it a try."

"Really?", Hacker asked.

"Yes, what you've got going for you is the idea – which is good, if it's thought through – and your energy. You're really selling yourself as someone that will deliver what he's promised."

"I'd certainly do that."

"Yes, I think you probably would," Mac agreed. "What you need to do is come up with answers to the questions people are going to ask: what it is, what it covers, what's the market, how many copies, at what price, and so on. Convince people you've thought it all through. A business plan, I suppose you could call it."

"I see," Hacker said. "But I have no idea how many copies you might be talking about, nor how much it would cost to get printed. Without that, I can't work out the price to sell it at."

"I can help with those. I'm used to dealing with printers. And you can get the number of copies the local papers sell from their mastheads. If it's going to be an insert, then the number's the same as the paper you go for. If it's a separate publication, and they're just distributing it to the newsagents, it's a lot less and you'll have to find some other way of coming up with a reasonable number of copies. You don't want to aim too small or the price will be more. Equally, though, you don't want to go for a large number of copies that never sell. That might help you to think about whether an insert is preferable as well."

"But do people my age buy the local paper?"

"Probably not," Mac said. "But you could use that as another selling-point. If they do start buying the paper, the paper not only sells more copies, but can up its advertising rates – might even attract different advertisers as well."

"I'm going to need some help and advice to think all this through."

"Well, I'm prepared to help," Mac said.

"I'd appreciate that - but why, what's in it for you?"

"We can talk about that if you want. We could come to a deal on any profits, or you could let me advertise for free in the listing, or we could probably come up with some other arrangement. I don't want to muscle in on your idea unfairly, but I am prepared to be a partner in it – if that's what you want."

"I think you can already see that I'm going to need some help with the business side of it. You provide that and we'll do a deal on any profits – that's the most straightforward. Then we both know where we stand."

"Fair enough," Mac said.

"So, what's next?", Hacker asked.

"You go away and come up with the basic proposal you want to go for. And then we'll talk again. We'll see what else needs adding and then we can decide who to approach. But I would suggest the *Evening News*. I know the editor and I am sure he would want to back this."

"OK, when? When can we meet again?"

"How about the end of the week? Say the same time on Friday? It's going to take you a day or two to pull it all together, and I'm in London on Wednesday and Thursday."

"Fine. See you then then."

They shook hands again, and Mac showed him back out through the foyer. The doors were open now and the lights were on in the box office, but the foyer was still empty.

"See you on Friday," Mac said. "Unless you change your mind, that is."

"I'll see you on Friday," Hacker said firmly.

Mac smiled at Hacker's departing back as he went off down the steps.

5

Riddler's Yard had a wide entrance on to the road. Once this had been barred by double five- or six-bar metal gates, but they had long since been removed. All that remained were the wooden uprights on either side of the entry through five-foot high walls.

When Euphony had first come across Birton Sodbury, she had missed Riddler's Yard completely. Even when she had the estate agent's details, she had driven past the gateway before she realised it was there.

The entrance led into a wide open space that might have been used as a stockyard. The left perimeter of this yard was made up of a collection of byres and barns that ran the full length from the wall at the front to the smaller wall that marked the end of the yard and the start of the house and its garden. Room enough to park twenty or thirty cars, Euphony thought.

Totally overgrown now but what might have been a garden at the front of the house ran the entire width of the yard. When the Riddlers lived there it had been used for growing vegetables. Manure from the yard was thrown over the wall to fertilise the plot and many of the vegetables went the other way to feed the animals. Sustainability in action long before the concept existed, let alone became professionalised, but second nature to farmers. In the right-hand corner of the garden wall was a small gate, with a path leading up that side of the house to the front door. Behind the house was another garden that had once been laid with lawns and flowerbeds. This too had gone to seed and it was no longer possible to distinguish where the lawns might have ended and paths or flowerbeds began.

The right-hand edge of the yard comprised a continuation of the five-foot high wall at the front. This extended about halfway back on that side. The remainder of this side of the yard looked over to the fields that had once belonged to the farm. It was fenced with half a dozen concrete posts at five yard intervals carrying three streams of wire. The run of wire was broken between the middle two sets of posts by a wooden gate that had come away from its top hinge and lay open, propped into the yard against its upright. A tin water-trough was half-hidden by this gate.

The house itself had three rooms across the yard side on both the ground and first floors, a wide hallway opening into the middle of the house from the one door at the side, and two larger rooms on both floors on the garden side of the house. Both the ground floor rooms on this side had wide french windows that opened on to a patio that ran the width of the house and bridged the space to where the lawns had once begun. The kitchen was located on the other side of the hallway from the front door, with the bathroom directly above it.

The symmetry of the house therefore ran between the ground and first floors rather than, as is more usual, either front to back or from side to side. This might have been disorienting had it not been so light and airy. Only the front door was on the north side, with the rooms overlooking the yard facing east, the kitchen and bathroom south, and the garden rooms west. This meant that it was quite feasible to track the sun round the house. It looked all ways at once. Euphony could see the advantages of the west-facing rooms on a summer evening.

The architecture was solid, without being over-powering. The house had been built almost two hundred years before, but not in a recognisably Georgian style. In medieval times, Euphony had learnt, the site had originally been a leper colony. Over the intervening years there had been three previous farmhouses that had been replaced as the owners changed and the farm grew.

Euphony was amazed that it had taken the Riddler family nearly three years to sell it. Hacker had been right when he had described it as almost derelict; even the most optimistic estate agent would have to concede that it was in need of total modernisation. On the other hand, Euphony had been equally correct to talk of its excellent location. This was true of its setting as well, but that had not been what she meant.

Birton Sodbury was about three miles from the nearest town. Until recently, this had been so removed from the pace of modern life that it had often been used as the setting for historical dramas by film and television companies. But it was now a prosperous market town, very proud of its new university and booming economy. While tourism was still the mainstay, a number of new technology companies had started up or relocated there in recent years. The surrounding area also had well-established farming and horse-racing communities. In short, it was one of those areas that had built on its existing wealth and natural advantages by embracing the opportunities of the nineties. Much of the population was now young, mobile and affluent.

Birton itself had once been on the main route out of the market town. But the by-pass had returned it to a quieter, more rural state. While this had reduced Hacker's trade at The Old Bell, Euphony expected it to prove a boost to her's.

Although Euphony planned to live at Riddler's Yard in the short-term, she didn't at this stage know whether this would remain the case for long. If she did stay, it would only be in a few rooms on the first floor.

There were both advantages and disadvantages in being on site, and she was going to see how things panned out before committing herself either way.

Euphony had spent ten years getting to this point. Having waited this long, she was prepared to take some decisions only as they needed to be taken. But, nevertheless, she was keen to get on with things as fast as possible.

It had been ten years of damned hard work. But now she had the cash not only to acquire the site (and it had taken her nearly a year of looking all over this part of England before she found Birton Sodbury and Riddler's Yard), but to employ an architect to draw up the plans and a surveyor to oversee the building work. She intended to do the job properly.

Euphony had first conceived the idea of an up-market restaurant as a route out of her previous occupation. In some ways it had been a natural extension from it; catering for human appetites, but in a legal way. While still at college in the early 1980s, she had worked for a while in a casino. With her looks and brains she was a natural croupier – easy to watch and fast with her hands, as well as with her head. Even just working two nights a week had quickly covered her overdraft and made her more than she got from the grant. When she left college, she stayed on to work at the casino through the summer. By the time she moved on she had seen at least three punters destroy their lives through their greed. One of them had been well up on the house, but kept going, thinking his luck would hold. By the end of the night he had lost the ten thousand he had won and another twenty thousand trying to win it back.

That was a heavy loss in a small provincial casino. The guy would probably spend the rest of his life regretting it.

What had surprised Euphony most was not that such greed existed; she had anticipated that. Rather she was amazed that it could be accompanied by such rank stupidity. A good gambler weighs the odds, doesn't bet more than he can afford to lose, and stops when he's ahead. A stupid one doesn't do any of these – either they have no judgement to suspend, or they jettison it in favour of greed, or they trust to a fair wind. But there is no luck in gambling. It's a matter of cool statistical calculation.

Euphony left the casino to take up a trainee accountant post with a major firm in London. She quickly became part of the office social scene. Indeed, within weeks of moving to London, she had progressed on from the group that went to the pub every night to the hard core that went on from the pub to the clubs.

Some of these clubs were extraordinarily sleazy. Often Euphony was the only woman present who wasn't a hostess. She didn't really know what she was doing there, other than being a good colleague and mixing with the few people she knew in London. What she didn't realise was that her colleagues didn't know what she was doing there either. Weren't the women expected to leave the pub early, if they went there at all?

She became a target for whispering behind her back – by the women as much as the men. And, when a couple of minor things went wrong on her accounts, she had become an easy target to blame. Within six weeks of starting she had been fired. As a trainee, she had no redress.

This left her in London, with a flat to keep up and knowing virtually nobody except her former colleagues. She tried to get a job as a croupier, but found there were none to be had. In desperation to pay the mortgage, she had responded to a small ad for escorts.

She went into this without any illusions. But she viewed it as a short-term move to get her back on her feet. Six years later she was still doing it and she could feel herself becoming harder and more embittered by the day. But the moment and motivation to enter a legitimate profession had long since passed. She realised that she would have to find another route out. And fast – she'd be thirty in three years.

It was at this point that she came up with the idea of the restaurant. Having been taken to most of the best ones in London over the previous six years, she felt she knew what made a successful one. But could she re-create it? It had taken her another ten years to get to the point where she could finally find out.

Having the restaurant as a goal enabled her to put some distance between Euphony the person and Euphony the call-girl. The restaurant became a justification for why she was doing what she was. This also allowed her a rationale for expanding her repertoire: the more she did, the more rapidly would her capital swell. She began to look on the johns as her backers. This made it easier to take, reducing her disenchantment and depersonalisation, but was somewhat ironic, given that if anyone was on their back, it was usually her.

She could see the humour in this. As she could in the fact that she now turned tricks as fast as she used to turn cards. Fast hands were still an asset.

6

When Hacker left the Exchange after meeting Mac, he went straight home and up to his room. He got out an old exercise book from school, tore out the used pages and began jotting down the suggestions that Mac had made: insert or separate publication?, number of copies?, printing costs?, number of pages?, distribution costs? Then he realised he'd have to add in other costs, including how much he thought he could pay himself. He tried out a dummy in terms of the information to include for each venue and a couple of different layouts. Was 'Who's Where When?' the best title he could come up with? It didn't immediately tell you that it was a guide to music venues. Should it say this? What would the cover look like? Did the title have a question mark at the end or not?

The more Hacker got into it, the more ideas came to him. Some of them he could resolve. Others he would have to ask Mac what he thought. He wanted to get as much of it sorted before Friday as possible, but he was going to need Mac's help and advice on several points.

Over the next three days Hacker spent hour after hour thinking through the various possibilities and trying out different versions.

"What are you doing up there all day?", his mother asked him on the Thursday.

"Working."

"Working on what? Why don't you work on getting a job?"

"I am. You'll see." And Hacker went back to his room.

"Dreamer," muttered his mother to herself.

By late on the Thursday evening Hacker had pulled all his thoughts together into one proposal. He was ready to talk it through with Mac.

When he eventually went to bed, Hacker found that he couldn't sleep. He wasn't nervous or anxious about what Mac would think of his efforts, but he was keen to find out. He was excited at the prospect of the meeting.

As a result, Hacker got up early and arrived at the Exchange over an hour before he was due to meet Mac. The doors were locked and it was too cold to wait outside, so he walked back and forth through the town, turning the proposal over in his mind, trying to anticipate the questions Mac would ask and checking the list of points Hacker wanted to ask him.

When Hacker got back to the Exchange, there was no sign of Mac outside. The doors were still closed. Hacker knocked repeatedly, but there was no answer. Hacker waited. But, as the minutes went by, he began to have doubts. Perhaps Mac had changed his mind; perhaps he had never really expected Hacker to turn up and had just been humouring him; he could have been the office boy for all Hacker knew. Worst of all, perhaps Mac had stolen the idea for himself. Even now the *Evening News* presses might be churning out the first edition of 'Mac's Guide to Manchester's Music' or something similar.

Hacker tried to put these thoughts out of his mind. After all, Mac had seemed genuine enough. But it became increasingly difficult once 10.00 arrived, half an hour after Mac had been due to meet him. Hacker didn't know what to do. Should he try ringing in case his knocking had not been heard? But if he went off to the phone box he might miss him altogether. Presumably Mac or someone would have to turn up by 10.30 when the box office was due to open?

Hacker would have been freezing cold by now, standing outside on the steps for nearly forty-five minutes, except that his anger and frustration were keeping him warm. Just as he was beginning to think he had been duped, he saw Mac hurrying up the street towards him.

"Sorry," Mac panted once he was near enough for Hacker to hear him. "The train back this morning was delayed. Come on in. You must be freezing waiting out here."

Hacker's anger abated, to be replaced by relief, but he still glowered as he followed Mac into the Exchange.

Mac apologised again as he ushered Hacker into the office.

"So, what have you decided?", Mac asked when they were both seated with a cup of tea in their hands.

Hacker showed Mac the dummy he had prepared and the overall proposal. He answered the queries Mac raised, and followed up the points on which he had wanted Mac's advice.

When they had been over it a couple of times, Mac was ready to give his verdict.

"Sounds great to me. I thought you'd come up with the goods. Is there anything else we need to cover or should I fix for us to meet the *Evening News*?"

"I can't think of anything else," Hacker said.

"OK," Mac said. "What's the time? Not bad – I'll try ringing now if you like."

When Mac rang the editor, Hacker got the impression that this was not the first time that they had discussed the idea of a listings magazine. Mac did too little explaining of what was involved for it to have been a new idea to the editor. The meeting was fixed for late that afternoon, when the final edition had gone to press.

"Do I need to do any more before we meet him?", Hacker asked.

"I don't think so. Just take him through it exactly as you have me. We should be able to answer any questions between us."

The editor was as enthusiastic about the proposal as Mac. He would no doubt have preferred an insert too, but was prepared to go with the separate publication. He offered some design support in return for the *Evening News* logo on the front cover.

Over the course of the next couple of weeks Mac and Hacker met with the paper's business managers and agreed the contractual details. This included providing Hacker with an office and secretary at the *Evening News*. Taking these costs on board, Hacker found that he could afford to pay himself £30 a week if all ten thousand copies sold. This was better than he had thought. His costings had worked out at £20 a week – more or less the same as he had been getting at Big Jim's. He still expected to make a small profit on top that he and Mac would split 70:30.

Hacker started working full-time from late November at the *Evening News* offices, and the first edition of 'Who's Where When?' came out in mid-December. It covered the week up to Christmas and that between Christmas and New Year. It had been heavily promoted in the *Evening News* throughout early December and Hacker could sense that it was going to take off. Having two weeks for the price of one should help too.

Hacker worked through Christmas to get the next edition ready for the beginning of the year. He had not been sure that starting just before Christmas was the best idea, but Mac and the editor had persuaded him that this was precisely the moment when young people would have even more time and money than usual to pursue their leisure interests. This might be coupled with a keener desire to get away from their families and the festivities. Things might be different in the new year when the weather could be worse and there would also be the competing attraction of the sales for people's pockets.

Hacker had remained sceptical, but he could see for himself that the copies were being sold very fast by the shops. When the returns came in at the beginning of January, 9,500 copies had been sold. It was not enough to make a profit, but no-one was down on the deal.

As things turned out, the magazine chimed exactly with its times, perhaps because of the way that Hacker had come up with the idea in the first place. His experience, and that of his friends, was clearly shared by many other young people who found it equally irritating. By late spring the number of copies being printed each week had already risen twice to a total of fifteen thousand. Hacker could have afforded to take on extra staff to do the detailed collection of the information, but he found he enjoyed doing it himself. He would also have had to check what anyone else did anyway, so he decided he might as well do it himself in the first place. This helped to keep him more closely in touch with readers' views and with the venues, both those he had included originally and those he had not. As Mac had predicted, other venues were by now clamouring to get in.

The continuous pace imposed by the weekly deadlines, and the growing sense of success, carried Hacker through the following weeks and months. He was hardly aware that time was passing. This was curious when he was working in a newspaper office, which by its nature marks the passing of time with daily events that seem momentous at the time, but are barely remembered a few days later. Partly this was because of Hacker's almost total focus on the magazine and its development, partly because each week's routine was much the same, and partly because his surroundings did mark the triumph of the ephemeral over the significant. It was all too easy to lose touch with the family events and relationships with friends that determine the rights of passage for most of us, and lay down the markers for our sense of past, present and future.

7

The Riddler family were delighted - and relieved - to have found a likely buyer at last and, though some token haggling was expected of them for form's sake, they were careful to do this only half-heartedly and briefly so as not to scare Euphony off. They need not have worried for once set on a course she was not easily deterred. Besides all the advantages were with her, a point she was not slow to make to the agent. The village was delighted that Riddler's Yard might be occupied once more – if only to keep imaginary squatters and vagrants out. Although the parish council put in a token objection to her initial application for planning permission on the grounds of increased traffic, this had barely delayed her obtaining it at all, and Riddler's Yard was soon her's at the price she had first offered. The local consensus was that an up-market restaurant beyond the means of most villagers was just what Birton Sodbury lacked – or at least that's what they told themselves. It should bring some local employment, an obvious good, especially for the young, and some of the farmers and landowners might expect to become suppliers, though this would never be more than a sideline that brought in a little extra money. Even if the clientele came from further afield, village vitality would be enhanced and other businesses, such as Hacker's pub and the riding school, might pick up other customers as well.

Euphony's main concern was to get the work underway as quickly as possible. The sooner the plans were approved and the builders in to convert the ground floor the better. She set up a camp bed in the one habitable room upstairs. This would have to act as her office while the work was being done. The rest of her things were stacked in the barn that didn't leak.

The crisp, cloudless morning augured well as Euphony stood out the front waiting for the surveyor to arrive. Hacker came into the yard.

"Hello again," he said. "I'd heard you'd moved in."

"Yes, last week. The builders start today."

"Well, you could hardly have a better morning weather-wise."

Euphony smiled. "If only it stays like this. But I'm in no rush."

"I'd have thought you wanted to get settled as quickly as possible."

"I do. But the building is just the start. I've got several other things to sort out as well."

Euphony assumed that Hacker would know she intended to open a restaurant. If nothing else he would have been consulted on the planning application given the possible impact on his trade at The Old Bell. But she thought she'd better check.

"You know I'm turning it into a restaurant, I take it?"

"Yes I do."

"And you don't mind?"

"Mind? Why should I mind? It's nothing to do with me what you decide to do. And, anyway, if it gets more people out here it's likely to be good for me too."

"I'm glad you see it that way. Not everybody would."

"Look Euphony – I wish you the very best of luck, I really do. In fact, I'll go further; if you think I can help in any way, let me know. I'd be delighted."

"I may well take you up on that."

"Do." He paused. "Have you decided what you're going to call it yet?"

"No, not finally. I can't decide whether to go for something pretentious or to keep it simple."

Hacker laughed. "Depends on the market you're trying to attract, I suppose."

"I'll probably go for something simple and rely on the chef to attract the market. Something like 'Euphony's' or even just 'Riddler's'. But I haven't decided yet.

Euphony wanted to include 'New' in the name somewhere if she could. But she didn't say this. On the one hand it encapsulated the fresh start she was trying to make. But on the other it might convey the wrong message. It sounded a bit like 'Under new management', and in her view that was often a mistake.

At that moment a car came into the yard.

"Ah, here's the surveyor at last," Euphony said.

"I'll leave you to it," Hacker said. "Good luck."

Hacker watched as Euphony walked round to the driver's side of the car. "Sorry I'm a bit late. Had trouble finding it," he heard the man say as he turned to leave the yard. At the gate Hacker looked back. Euphony was in deep conversation with the man, pointing to various features of the building, long a farmhouse but soon to be something else.

That evening Euphony came into The Old Bell. "How's it going?", Hacker asked when she came up to the bar.

"Not bad for the first day I suppose," she said. "They've taken up all the ground floor and knocked a couple of the walls down."

"That's good going. If they're as fast at putting things up, it won't take long at all."

Euphony smiled. "It'll be a couple of months. This is the easy bit."

"Anyway, what can I get you?"

"Oh, I don't want anything to drink - not at the moment anyway. What I was wondering was whether I could ask a favour."

"Fire away."

"They've had to turn the water off. So I wondered if I could have a bath here?"

"Of course," Hacker said. "Come through and I'll show you where it is."

"That's great. Thanks. I'll go back and get my things first."

Hacker was relieved. "That'll give me some time to clear up."

When Euphony returned, the bar was still empty. She sat down and waited for Hacker. He came back in a couple of minutes later.

"OK, it's a bit more presentable now. Come through."

Hacker led Euphony into the kitchen at the back of the bar. "This way." He opened the door in the corner that gave directly on to the staircase. She followed him up to the first floor. As she expected, the bathroom door was right next to the top of the stairs, looking out over the back of the pub.

"You'll have to excuse the colour scheme," Hacker said. "Not my choice of green. I keep meaning to change it, but never quite seem to get round to doing it.

"It is a bit bright, isn't it?", Euphony said.

"That's an understatement. Lurid, even livid, would be a better word."

Hacker showed her how the shower worked and then left her to it. Euphony locked the door and ran the bath. As she waited for it to fill, she looked in the bathroom cabinet. There was nothing unusual in the contents, but Euphony was surprised at how meticulously tidy and clean it was.

When Euphony came down an hour later, Hacker was in the kitchen.

"Everything all right?", he asked.

"Fine," she said. "Thanks very much. I appreciate it."

"No problem. You're welcome to use it any time."

"You're very kind."

Hacker smiled. "Look, I was just fixing something to eat. Do you want some?"

"What about your customers?"

"Haven't got any at the moment. Often don't on a Monday and if they're not here by ten they don't get in at all. I'll be closing up in a few minutes."

"Ok, then, yes I would," Euphony said. "Thanks again. After all this you'll have to be the first guest when the restaurant opens."

"Fair enough," Hacker said.

"Is there anything I can do to help?"

"Well you could get us something to drink. I'll have a bottle of Pils."

Euphony went through to the bar and returned with the Pils and a vodka and tonic for herself. Handing the Pils to Hacker she sat down at the huge oak table in the middle of the kitchen. She watched him for a couple of minutes as he moved around the kitchen, preparing the food. If she was appraising him, he appeared not to be aware. When he stopped for a moment to take a drink, she asked him what had brought him to Birton.

"Nothing in particular," Hacker said. "I just seemed to end up here."

"That sounds like you don't want to tell me."

"Do you really want to know? It's not a very interesting story."

Euphony nodded.

"As you can guess, it was an escape. Well, not exactly an escape - and certainly not an escape from anything I'd done," he added. "More a way of avoiding what might have happened, what I might have done, if I hadn't got away."

He looked at Euphony in an attempt to gauge her reaction. She was waiting for him to continue.

"Look, you're the first person I've told here, so I'd appreciate it if it went no further."

"I'm not going to tell anybody," Euphony said. "Apart from anything else, I don't know anybody to tell. But, even if I did, I wouldn't."

So Hacker told her how he'd started 'Who's Where When?' in the early seventies. "It began well and just went from strength to strength. Both met a need and to some extent created one. After a couple of years I was still running the Manchester operation, but we'd also started up in Leeds. Mac was running that. So by then we were full partners. It was taking off there too and we had the lifestyle to match, fast cars, parties, you know the sort of thing."

"Yes, indeed I do. Or at least I can imagine it," Euphony added.

"I was still in my early twenties and it looked like life was just going to get better and better. Which it did, for quite a long time."

"So what went wrong?"

"Things began to go wrong when Mac persuaded me we should buy this club in Leeds. At the time it seemed the right thing to do. It was doing well under its previous owners, but was reasonably priced for reasons I won't go into. It gave us another angle on the market and so on. Only trouble was we needed to find someone we could trust to run it. We tried a couple of managers, but they simply weren't up to it. Eventually, we put my wife in."

"I thought you must be married," Euphony said.

"I was, but not for long."

"What happened?"

"Quite simple really. I was in Manchester most of the time. Mac was in Leeds. She needed help to run the club and while she could ring me up, and did a lot at the start, he was on hand. Things just developed from there. Inevitable really. She'd known him about as long as she'd known me."

"How did you find out?"

"She told me – though I pretty well knew by then anyway. Trouble was, she told me in the club, we had a flaming row and the bouncers threw me out. Threw me out of my own club!"

"So was that when you came to Birton?"

"No, that was just the start. A couple of nights later the club was torched and of course I was the prime suspect. Fortunately, I was in London on business at the time and was able to prove it. But the police clearly thought I was behind it, even if I hadn't actually done it. It certainly gave the insurance company enough of a reason not to pay up. That was when I decided it was time to move on."

"So what happened to the business?"

"I sold my share to Mac. I tried other people first but no-one was going to give me as much as him. That gave me enough to buy this place."

8

From Euphony's standpoint the local council seemed to delight in putting obstacles in the way - as if regulations were designed to disable rather than enable development. Building control's requirements might delay, though with an understandable and therefore acceptable purpose, but planning's expectations were much more difficult to fathom. It was not just that they appeared labyrinthine, they were not even applied consistently in Euphony's opinion. She might be led to believe one thing only to have it overturned or reversed at the next hurdle. Even with Hacker's help 'pause law', as Euphony characterised it, almost made her give up. The rationale for building control she could appreciate, some of the planning hurdles she encountered were much less necessary. Parking and the number of places she had to provide were one element, but she had to give assurances on noise, re-assurances on opening hours, fulfil licensing requirements and demonstrate that the restaurant would meet environmental health standards. There were also a lot of employment, health and safety, and training regulations and requirements that she had to familiarise herself with.

"This had better be worth it," she thought. She had expected it to be complex, and that it would be complicated to navigate her way through, but if she had known at the start the demands that would be made of her even before she opened, she might not have pursued it at all. Every ounce of her determination was required to persist, though being bloody-minded helped too.

Eventually, the sign went up over the entrance, another on the wall by the gate and she had even managed to get a couple of direction posts at the top of the road and the start of the village. Another on the by-pass would have been ideal but that was more than the planners were prepared to countenance. Despite her reservations about the word 'New', and the temptation of 'Riddler's Restaurant' or even just 'Riddler's', she had decided to call it 'The New Place'. Recruitment was complete, or at least sufficient to begin with, and the whole village was invited to the opening night. They would not all come of course, but it was too good an opportunity to get the village on her side for the positive PR opportunity to be missed. As importantly from Euphony's point of view, it was a chance to test the systems before the paying customers arrived. Many villagers would be curious, others attracted by the free meal, and if some were looking forward to a disaster on their doorstep, others would be hoping for the best.

Meeting and greeting was one of Euphony's strengths, making people feel welcome without the necessity for a formal speech or tour of the premises. She introduced herself to each party as they arrived, showed them to their table and called forward their particular waiter from those hovering at the edge of the restaurant. Checking that the guests had no initial questions, she returned to the foyer to repeat the exercise with the next group. Quiet at first the restaurant soon warmed up with the buzz of conversation and palpable anticipation.

"People's sexuality is their own affair," a daughter told her parents at one table.

"And presumably that of their partner?", her father asked.

"Or possibly that of their partners," her mother added in a knowing way. Her husband looked at her quizzically but did not respond - though whether because he was nonplussed or feared a trap was not clear.

Perhaps he had decided that, despite his daughter's sophistication and the rich elegance of the restaurant this was not the time or place to risk finding out more than he wanted to know.

Euphony could tell that these diners had been attracted from the nearby town, or even further afield, by the opportunity for a new experience that might satisfy their avant-garde sensibilities, if only briefly. The conversations on tables occupied by local residents were much more basic, especially that of the archetypal Old Sod Colonel Coward, his wife Cecilia and their friends from the golf club Mr and Mrs Bartholomew Bogey. She, a rather large and now a non-playing member, having exceeded the capabilities of even the best-tuned buggy, was called Mrs Bogey to her face and 'Double Bogey' behind her back.

"We finished our starter twenty minutes ago," said Cecilia Coward, "but nobody's come to collect our plates, let alone apologise."

"It's not good enough," whined Colonel Coward.

"I've tried to attract the waiter's attention but he's ignoring me," said Bartholomew Bogey.

"You need to do it like this ... WAITER!" bellowed Double Bogey. The restaurant fell silent.

Euphony hurried over. "You have a problem?", she asked.

"It's half an hour or more since we finished our first course," Mrs Bogey exaggerated, "and we're still waiting for the main."

"It's not good enough," added Colonel Coward, a refrain he had made his own.

"I'm very sorry," said Euphony. "We are having some difficulties but that's no excuse for your waiter not collecting the plates or explaining the situation. I'll speak to him. Can I get you another bottle of wine in the meantime?"

"Yes please," said Cecilia. "We seem to be getting to the bottom of this one."

Euphony took their plates away into the kitchen and almost immediately afterwards the waiter came out to remove the bread crumbs from their table, apologising as he did so.

"This might be a ruse to make sure we drink more," observed Bartholomew Bogey. "Perhaps they think we'll forget the poor service and it will cost us more anyway."

Despite Euphony's promise and Hacker's intentions, he had not managed to find cover for the pub that night. For a while he had thought of closing for the evening, but this became less feasible as some of his older regulars made it plain that they had never been in a restaurant in their lives and were not about to start now. "All front and no knickers," as Tom had put it, mangling the customary definition of a tart in his pointed but unconsciously apt way. Closing would have had the advantage of bringing the village up short, for Hacker was aware he risked becoming a feature of the local landscape, taken for granted as part of the village furniture like the post box, but it was not the sort of thing the 'Old Sods' would readily forget. In the end The Old Bell stayed open and Hacker missed The New Place's opening night. He could tell Euphony was disappointed when he sent his apologies but as a fellow business person she understood his reasons, especially in a small place where reputation and image went hand in hand. She would have to tell him how it went instead.

9

"It went fine," Euphony assured Hacker when she came into The Old Bell at lunchtime the next day. "Some people had to wait a while to be served but the kitchen worked smoothly - staff and kit - better than I'd dared hope in fact."

"So very well really given this was a first run-out and with a full house too?"

"Yes, I suppose so." She paused, "I know I should be talking it up rather than worrying about the downside, but some of the locals take a bit of getting used to."

"That's putting it mildly," he laughed. "You probably won't see most of them again though."

"Some we won't, but probably the ones for whom this was always going to be a never-to-be-repeated experience even if they could afford it. They were no trouble anyway, but the most offensive table, and certainly the most drunk, were the golf club crew. They're bound to be back. Indeed, one looked as though she specialises in second helpings."

"That'll be Double Bogey," said Hacker. "Her husband's all right on his own, especially in comparison, but tends to follow her lead too readily. Perhaps it's his only way to a quiet life - or at least a quieter one."

"That's just how they came across, and they acted as though they owned the place," Euphony said.

"Much of Birton Sodbury they probably do and they've lived here a long time so the little that doesn't actually belong to them may feel as though it does. Were the Cowards with them?"

"An old bloke who kept telling me and everybody else 'It wasn't good enough'?"

"That's the Colonel all right but it's his wife you've got to watch out for. No doubt who's in charge though Cecilia lets him think he is."

"Sozzled Cecilia on this occasion."

"Really? Rumour has it that she often is, but rarely in public," Hacker said.

"Some people mellow after a few but I suspect she's not one of them?"

"I've never had to find out fortunately. The Old Bell is beneath her and Double Bogey, though their husbands sometimes come in. Probably 'any port in a storm' as far as they're concerned. Anyway, enough of them, what's next for you?"

"We open for real next Saturday. We've had a few bookings but it's bound to be a bit quieter. I don't suppose you'll be able to make that either?"

"No, I'm afraid not - though I will try to get in sometime soon. Evenings are quieter during the early part of the week."

"It may be a while before we can afford to open then. An empty restaurant is never a good advertisement so Wednesdays and Fridays may be next."

"That's just when I'm busiest too, I'm afraid. People must be ready to get out of the house by Wednesday but on Thursdays they manage to wait for the weekend."

"OK but don't leave it too long."

10

A month later and Hacker was relieved when another quiet night in The Old Bell was redeemed when his first customer of the evening came in. Hacker had never seen the man before and didn't recognise his fractured and accented English when he asked for a double brandy.

"There you go," said Hacker taking the ten pound note. He was still getting the change from the till when the man asked for another. Hacker refilled the man's glass, looking at him quizzically and resisting the temptation to suggest he take the next one a bit slower.

"I'm Hacker," he said. "Are you passing through?"

"No, I live here - for moment at least," said the man. "I'm Kristof, the chef at restaurant. You know it, round the corner?" He put down his drink and he and Hacker shook hands.

"Yes, I do. But I've never been in so I didn't recognise you. Have you been there since it opened?"

"Yes, apart from owner I was first there. Two months already though I've been in Britain for three years."

"Where are you from?"

"Small town in Poland. You won't have heard of it, just over German border from Dresden."

"The south of Poland then?"

"Yes, or south-west really. North of Prague and Czech border too."

"Not as quiet as Birton Sodbury, surely?"

"Certainly larger - a town rather than big village. Otherwise much the same."

"So you feel at home then?"

"Yes - and no. I did but need to work more than two days a week."

"It's bound to build up," Hacker said. "Seems popular enough when it's open."

"Yes, I am good chef and people now know that. But it's not open enough and owner got some funny ideas."

"Euphony Blurr? I know her and know she wants to make it a success."

"You a friend?" Kristof asked.

"I wouldn't go that far. Not close anyway but we've met a few times since she moved here. I think she knows she's taking a huge gamble but if anyone can pull it off she can."

"Yes, I thought so too. That's what made me move here. But I'm beginning to wonder."

Hacker was not about to betray Euphony but he would hardly have been human, let alone a fellow business person, almost a competitor, had this not aroused his curiosity. Hacker was about to ask Kristof what he meant but Tom and another regular came in so, after pulling their pints and getting Kristof another brandy, Hacker decided to leave it at that for now. He didn't want to be misunderstood by the increasingly inebriated Kristof or risk the conversation being misinterpreted as disloyalty to Euphony. He certainly didn't want it relayed back to her in a garbled form. Or for it to find its way to the Old Sods, as it might if Tom misheard or embellished it in the hope of levering some prestige, or better still, some refreshment out of the senior residents of the village. Double Bogey and Cecilia Coward had more than enough wiles to winkle it out of Tom - and he would be only too delighted to tell them what they wanted to hear. Either husband could be despatched to provide Tom with his liquid recompense and would be pleased to act as the go-between in such circumstances. An hour in The Old Bell was an hour away from domestic expectations and, of course, they would have to keep Tom company. They could hardly buy him a pint and leave.

When he next saw Euphony, Hacker congratulated her on the restaurant's growing popularity. "Yes, it is going well," she said, "Fridays as well as Saturdays, but I'm not sure we're quite doing well enough yet to risk Wednesdays as well. We haven't built up a wide enough profile and I'm not sure I could cover the losses for long."

"Not bad for six weeks though. People think starting up is easy whereas sustaining it is something else. In my experience both are tough and it's better to build gradually - like you are." Hacker paused. "I met your chef a couple of weeks ago by the way."

"Good," said Euphony. "I'm glad to hear he's getting out and about at last. It was pretty full on for the first few weeks, but he's a big part of the success so the more he feels part of the village the better. Did you manage to talk to him much?"

"Only briefly. Enough to find out where he comes from and why he chose here. He was clearly attracted by your plans, but we didn't talk long enough to find out any more."

Hacker had no reason to undermine Euphony's faith in Kristof and was even less inclined to do so. His natural instincts were constructive, building bridges if he could but at any rate not weakening them.

"If only all the staff were as enlightened as Kristof, my life would be a lot simpler."

This was intriguing, Hacker thought. "How do you mean?"

"Some are far from being as flexible and accommodating. That's one of the things that worries me about opening on Wednesdays," Euphony explained. "Many of the staff seem to have added Fridays and Saturdays at the restaurant on to their existing commitments and they might not be as ready to do the same on Wednesdays."

"Perhaps they wouldn't be able to. There might be benefits in having different staff then, do you think?"

"Except for recruitment and training there might be. I'm not sure I could cope with that again so soon after the previous round. Nor might it be feasible for one day a week."

"Agency temps?"

"Too risky. It only has to go badly once for the consequences to be out of all proportion. Even knock-on effects for the Friday and Saturday custom perhaps. You'll know that from your club."

Hacker winced. "Very different circumstances, but I know what you mean." Euphony had never presumed on his disclosure previously and Hacker was surprised to find it had this result. The pain had soon disappeared at the time and he thought he was long over the humiliation, raw as it had remained for a while, but clearly not. "It was only a suggestion anyway," Hacker continued, "and clearly not a very helpful one."

"You may be right though. I'll give it some thought."

Hacker found himself busier than usual over the next month and barely gave Euphony or her restaurant a second thought. Strangely enough it was Bartholomew Bogey who asked him one evening if he'd heard.

"Heard what?" Hacker asked.

"About New Place. The Council have closed it down. Must have had too many complaints or found a filthy kitchen or something."

"Are you sure? It was going so well too."

"No, it never fitted in here. All those city types in their fast cars driving around trying to find it with no consideration for anyone else."

"Must have been more than that. A few trivial complaints about traffic would hardly be enough."

"There have been more than a few complaints I can tell you. The Cowards had a meeting about the problems a little while ago."

Hacker had guessed that the Old Sods would be massing, seeing Euphony as a threat to their way of life and carefully guarded status quo. But Euphony would not be one to under-estimate them, especially as he had tried to warn her.

As soon as he could, Hacker went round to see for himself and indeed there was a sign on the door saying "Closed until further notice". But it wasn't signed by the Council, only by Euphony herself. Hacker tapped on the window and eventually Euphony opened the door.

"We're shut," she said.

"I can see that. But why? Can I come in?"

Euphony let him in and followed him through to the bar area.

"I've just heard from Bogey that the Council have closed you down," he said.

Euphony laughed, "Well, it's not as bad as that - though it might as well be. I've had to sack Kristof and until I get another chef there's no point in opening."

"What happened? I know he liked a drink but that goes with the territory."

"That was fine. It never stopped him doing his job. Nor was it too much of a problem when he wanted to open on other nights and neither I nor the staff were ready for it. But after he'd finished last Saturday he got his car out to go elsewhere - or at any rate tried to."

"You mean he was stopped?"

"I wish he had been. No, he never got that far. In trying to get his car out of the yard he drove into one of the customer's and, as far as I can make out, then panicked and hit another three."

"Good grief."

"Fortunately nobody was hurt, not even Kristof. No-one seems to have witnessed it either but we certainly heard it. Not the first crash perhaps but the conversation in the restaurant simply ceased with the second and the others could be heard as clear as anything. That was when people started to panic."

"I don't know what to say. No wonder you had to sack him."

"The police took him away and apart from collecting his things I've not seen him since. The worst thing though is not that, though there won't be many available chefs as good as him, not even that I'm responsible for the insurance claims - public liability, you see - and that the premium will go up hugely. No, the worst thing is what it will have done to the reputation. None of those customers will be back, even if their car was not one of those hit."

"What about the other staff? You need to keep them if you can."

"They're sticking with me for the moment - or at least they say they are. But it will only be a matter of time once I can't pay them. The only positive is that other jobs round here aren't easy to come by."

"No, there is another - though it might be of limited consolation at the moment."

"What's that?" Euphony asked.

"Well I'm not sure how, but inadvertently you seem to have wrong-footed the Old Sods. For some reason they think they are responsible for the closure and even more strangely they don't seem to know the real reason."

"Perhaps the Council were about to act but Kristof got there first?"

"No, if that was the case you'd know by now. Just shows how arrogant they are that they think they're the cause."

"It did happen late at night but I'm still surprised that they haven't heard somehow."

"There can't have been anyone from the village around and the staff either don't mix with the Old Sods or know it's not in their own interests to let it get out."

Euphony smiled, the first time she had done so since Hacker arrived. "You may be right."

"The important thing now is to make sure they don't find out for as long as possible. They'll leave you alone if they think they've brought this about. The longer they're kept in the dark the better. That is, assuming you want and can afford to re-open?"

"I can't afford not to. Nearly everything I've got is wrapped up in this place. But I'm not sure I've got the energy to tackle it right now. Not unless you were able to give me a hand."

"I'm not sure about that," Hacker said. "I don't have much time and being your own boss is very different to working with someone else."

"You wouldn't have to do more than you wanted, I promise. But you're the nearest to a friend I've got and without your support I'm not sure I could pull it off."

"I'd like to help, Euphony, I really would, but I'll need to think about it if it goes beyond someone to bounce ideas off. Moral support you can rely on, but actual assistance might be something else."

"I won't tell you to take your time because that's something I don't have. Anything would be better than nothing - and you'll have to tell me if I'm asking for more than support."

"I don't mind you asking," Hacker said. "But expecting you can forget."

11

Despite their previous conversation, and the subsequent appeals that had got her nowhere, Euphony continued to hope that Hacker would become actively engaged. She might have resorted to feminine subterfuge but she would not convince him (or anyone) of her helplessness and dependence on male assistance, and was not about to go down the route of sexual enticement. She had put that behind her and she suspected anyway that he was immune to such blandishments where she was concerned. If anything was going to happen between them, it would have done by now. Especially when Hacker and The Old Bell had been her only source of respite and refreshment before the restaurant opened. The only option left to her was to cut him a deal in the hope that this would re-activate his business instincts. If he helped her get the restaurant back on its feet, he could have a share of any profits. In effect he would become a sleeping partner, ironically and in a different, more explicit sense, the role she had once occupied. She was aware that she would have to put this carefully to him. Apart from his in-built resistance, she was in effect offering him the role that Mac had taken in the listings business. Whatever else, she would have to suggest a different split of the profits so that he was not automatically reminded.

"I've been thinking about how long this is taking," Euphony said to Hacker one evening. "Recruiting a new chef after only a few months was always going to be difficult, but whether because of the location or the name it's proving even more tedious than I thought it might."

"Well, you might want to change the location but you can't. Anyway, why give the Old Sods the satisfaction?"

"What about the restaurant name then? That might help."

"Yes, you could try that I suppose. There'll be the signs to change as well as all your paperwork and menus, so it won't be cheap. But your advertising has been mainly word of mouth so far and a few local papers, so changing that won't cost any more. And you might try the internet this time too. That will add to the design costs but websites are the coming thing and once it's up there it won't cost much to update. You might even be able to do it yourself."

Euphony could sense that these ideas had captured Hacker's interest. It would be up to her to keep him motivated if she wanted the ideas to continue flowing. "I'll think about the name."

"You'll also need to think about the image you want to convey. That's partly about the style and design so that it's the same on the signs, the menu, the website. But there's no point going for something which communicates one thing while the restaurant itself does something entirely different."

"You mean that image and reality have to match? At its most basic, there's no point giving it a French name if the chef prefers to cook Italian?"

"That's right. It all has to tie together. 'The New Place' left things open but you might want to try something different this time or your chef's preferences might force you to."

"There's a lot to think about," Euphony said.

"Yes, but at least the Old Sods don't seem to have got wind of it as yet - not as far as I can tell anyway - so you have a bit more time to pace yourself."

"I still want you to be in on this."

"I know. But I don't. I'm happy for you to test things out but I'm not prepared to get in any deeper than that."

"I understand. But I wanted to ask if you might at least help me interview chefs. I'll give them all the practical tests together with some of the other staff. But having someone else in the interviews to help me judge character would be a big help. It would only be a few hours at most."

"I'll think about it," Hacker said, "but I'm not promising anything."

12

Hacker did give it some thought, and then some more, but Euphony had been right to assume that he would ultimately be unable to resist. Few chefs had applied, Euphony had culled these further and even fewer turned up to the interviews. The three that were left were a reasonable field but none of them looked to have as much promise as Kristof. On the other hand, they might not have his demolition derby skills either. Kristof's departure had reminded Hacker of the Saki[1] aphorism: 'He was a good cook as cooks go, and as good cooks go he went.' But it was a fair bet, though Hacker couldn't remember the details, that Saki had been referring to a more restrained and low-key departure. Kristof had stamped a new meaning on the phrase 'giving your customers something to remember'.

Hacker had suggested that the chefs be invited on different days so that they could meet some of the staff and use the kitchen. This would test their skills and give the remaining staff the opportunity to provide feedback, involving them in the process. Each of the chefs would be asked to prepare the same fish dish and then whatever sweet they thought best demonstrated their talents. Instead of waiting, the staff could supervise the kitchen and do some tasting, adding their views to Hacker's and Euphony's.

It was while they were waiting to interview the third chef after she had finished in the kitchens that Euphony made a suggestion.

---

[1] Pseudonym of the short-story writer Hector Hugh Munro (1870-1916)

"You know I couldn't have done this without you, and it's made a huge difference to the staff seeing you interested as well. How about staying involved? Not on a daily basis - I know you won't commit to that, and it might be too much for me as well. No, I was thinking more of a watching brief, a consultant if you like, to make suggestions about what needs to change and how."

"I really don't know, Euphony," Hacker said. "I admit I've enjoyed helping with this bit but it might be as well to leave it at that."

"Come on. What have you got to lose? You can pull out at any time if you decide it's not for you. But you know I need someone to keep me on the straight and narrow and nobody else would be half as good."

"So, I could be your S&N adviser?" Hacker laughed.

"You can be my S&M adviser if you like - as long as you say 'yes'."

"No, I don't think I'll go that far. It might not look too good in your business plan either."

"You could have a proper contract so that's there's no question about getting out when you want and half the profits. How about that?" Euphony asked.

"A contract might be going too far. And you haven't even got the restaurant going again yet so talking about profits might be a bit premature."

"I was thinking of a contract that rather than bind you in with a notice period or on a rolling basis makes it clear that if you want to get out you can - there and then if you choose." She looked at him hopefully. "And half the profits if - when - the restaurant gets back on its feet as a going concern."

"OK, I'll have to go for that. No reason not to and you're very persuasive - but no long-term promises," Hacker said. "Now let's finish these interviews. But nobody else in the village must know about this. It's got to stay just between me and you."

"I understand," said Euphony.

"No, I need to be clear. I'm not just thinking about the Old Sods and the havoc they could wreak at The Old Bell as well as here if they decided to. I'm thinking that you're the boss here and the staff and everybody in the village needs to see you as such. Nobody questions it."

"Don't worry. That's not something I'm ever going to compromise on. I need help and advice not a take-over."

"You know I wouldn't be interested in a take-over anyway. No, I was thinking more of how other people might misunderstand, perhaps even deliberately exploit any opening they thought might be in their interests."

"Thanks Hacker," Euphony said. "You're right of course - and I appreciate you saying it. Makes it clear where we both stand."

"Are you ready for me now?" said chef 3 as she came out of the kitchen.

"Yes, Natasha, we are," Euphony said. "We'll taste your cooking in the kitchen first and then come back here to ask you some questions."

13

Perhaps partly because she had been interviewed last, or because it was the taste of her cooking that lingered longest, though in all probability because she was able to commit to an early start, Euphony and Hacker agreed to offer Natasha the job. Indeed, so enthusiastic were they that even though there were only the two of them it would be appropriate to describe their decision as unanimous. She didn't hesitate either and agreed to start in a week. Euphony was careful to let the other candidates know how close the decision had been, not because it was but in case Natasha departed as quickly as Kristof and she needed another replacement fast.

Euphony set herself the testing target that the restaurant should re-open the week after the new chef started. This allowed some time for Natasha to familiarise herself with the kitchen and re-shape the menu according to her skills and the ingredients that were still useable, and for the staff to be re-oriented to the new situation. Critically, though, Euphony needed the cash flow to right itself as soon as possible. The overhaul included a change of name to 'New Yew'. Hacker was never sure where this had come from for there were no prominent trees on the site, and, if there had been, Euphony would have made sure they were cut down. Nevertheless, she had clearly been pondering it for a while.

To re-brand in less than a fortnight with all the re-writing of menus and new signage that was required might well have proved too much but, as it happened, most of the staff helped Euphony through it, increasing their belief in, even ownership of, the new concept. Some no doubt did so because they judged it in their interests, others because they empathised with Euphony's ordeal and could see she needed their assistance. The upshot was that when the restaurant re-opened on time, and the few diners were appreciative, the overall team bond was reinforced - or, to put it the other way round, possibly the stronger bond ensured that it went well. Had the Old Sods attempted to scupper things at this stage, the New Yews would have been ready to confront them, fired up and itching for a fight. That the Old Sods kept away might have been due to behind-the-scenes intriguing, a diplomatic silence or, more likely, incompetence. Double Bogey's arrogance could blind her to the activities of others, while Cecilia Coward may just have been *hors de combat*, in other words too inebriated, when it mattered most.

Once again the restaurant recovered as the weeks went by, the trade building up even better than before. One thing that had been overlooked, first in the rush and then in the euphoria, was the contract Euphony had promised Hacker. He was not unduly worried to begin with as he knew she had more pressing matters to attend to. After all if these went wrong there would be nothing to contract about. But as the weeks changed into months he wondered if Euphony was deliberately prevaricating. The novel approaches to nouvelle cuisine that Natasha introduced had won both customers nearby and admirers further afield. Potential diners who might have been wary given the restaurant's history had been unable to resist, becoming actual ones as its reputation spread. The restaurant's future then looked assured when it was taken up by the foodies and began to get rave reviews, its initial popularity locally embellished by a regional profile and prominence that turned it into preference. It had become the venue to visit. The next step was to open more often.

Euphony had relied on Hacker's advice, and in many instances his direct support, to get this far, but now that the restaurant was maintaining itself, his assistance would largely be behind the scenes. But it would be no less important for being less obvious, even in some respects hidden. The Old Bell provided an outlet for much of the village to voice their views. Most of his customers could not afford, and in many instances would not wish, to be among the restaurant's clientele, but they bore it no ill-will either and were prepared to accept Hacker's positive comments at face value. If he commended it, they had no reason to argue and the few that did were often going through the motions to pass the time, much as they had previously debated the rights and wrongs of angling permits. The 'New Place' might have lapsed into controversy and disappeared as fast as it emerged, but the 'New Yew' had settled down and was well on the way to becoming a tolerated, and in some quarters accepted, part of the village. Hacker did not delude himself though that the same would be true of the Old Sods. They might not have anything to object to at the moment but they were certainly keeping a look-out for the first infringement to complain about. In the meantime they kept up a grumbling bleat which Hacker did his best to counter.

Despite having played a part in revitalising the restaurant, both directly and by keeping most of the village on-side, Hacker suggested that he withdraw and leave Euphony to it. He expected her to agree and was surprised when she did not. He was even more surprised, though agreeably so, when this prompted her to produce the contract she had promised. Not quite half the profits, but Hacker had never expected that and his 40% share would still be enough to keep him interested. Euphony had taken advice that she should not put Hacker on the same basis as herself. She had put the capital in and, while his business acumen had been critical to the re-launch, if they fell out in the future there might be a long legal tussle about ownership if the contract implied equal shares. The contract was explicit that Hacker had no rights beyond this share of profits, but this might not stop lawyers disputing it in the courts for years. Hacker accepted Euphony's explanation for he appreciated that one certainty was that it would be the lawyers who would benefit if it came to this. Dickens had written *Bleak House* about the ability of the legal profession to drag matters out, procrastinating year after year, all the while draining away the disputed funds into their own pockets. Hacker had as little appetite for this prospect as Euphony.

He began to realise why Euphony had been keen to keep him involved. Hacker was becoming increasingly concerned about elements of Euphony's business practices. These were clearly creative but not always legal. Like many people running small businesses, Euphony paid attention to the issues confronting her at that moment, having neither the time nor the energy to act on those matters that could be put off till tomorrow. Besides which, the unnecessary hurdles put in her way by the local council when she was first setting up had reinforced her contempt for what she judged superfluous bureaucracy and red tape. If she didn't understand the rationale, as far as she was concerned there wasn't one. Her natural inclination was to act first and think later, an approach that sometimes served her well, but when her instincts were at odds with the legal requirements as much time, and sometimes more money, might have to be expended subsequently to right the situation.

It was Euphony's misfortune, if that is the right term, to come up against the immigration campaigns being mounted by all the main political parties. Nationally, some put it in terms of 'English jobs for English workers'; others in terms of the exploitation of immigrants. In rural areas such as Birton Sodbury, however, there was a dislike of foreigners taking jobs that supposedly would have gone to locals otherwise. This was a relentless undercurrent wherever jobs were few and far between and often seasonal. In the most extreme cases it could easily shade into scapegoating, with the immigrants blamed not just for unemployment but for all the ills of the area. In many cases these might have started centuries ago, but the facts were no match for the emotions. What was at best chauvinism, and in the worst cases racism, could be conveniently veiled under a banner of patriotism.

Faced with this political onslaught from above, and a popular one from below, the pressure was on the authorities to demonstrate that their area was squeaky clean, or if not above reproach was being cleansed. Inevitably, the spotlight focussed on the New Yew - possibly something that would have happened anyway, but almost certainly hastened by a nudge from the Old Sods. As Hacker had realised, some of the kitchen staff did not have the proper papers and were poorly paid, barely and not always at minimum wage levels. In addition, suppliers often had to wait a long time before their bills were met. This made the restaurant vulnerable to official scrutiny and ultimately to loss of trade. No customers were wilfully going to put themselves at odds with the authorities, let alone the politicians. No matter how good the food, it simply wasn't worth it.

14

It was clear to Euphony, as it was to Hacker, that she was not the person to tackle the issues the authorities raised. She wanted to see matters resolved as fast as possible but her head-down, no holds barred style was not the way to do it. In this instance her strengths might prove her weaknesses and this was not the time to find out. Or, to adopt the fashionable political parable, if you hadn't fixed the roof while the sun was shining, it was not a good idea to attempt it in the midst of a downpour. Even if Euphony was able to temper her approach, she lacked the patience required and, even if she appreciated the expectations, would she be able to implement the detail? Neither of them thought so. Furthermore, her history of conflict with the local authority over planning preceded her and this was not the moment to test whether her hackles were capable of rising higher than their's. Being exceptional front of house with the customers, as Euphony was, would make no difference in these negotiations. She could be as innovative as Hacker, perhaps more so in some respects, but being a good employer demanded a completely different skill-set. And being seen by the authorities to comply would be hampered by the acrimony she radiated when questioned. Hacker had the capacity to deflect confrontation, channelling scrutiny to a satisfactory conclusion. Euphony knew as well as he that these were not characteristics she had developed and there was no time to learn now.

So Euphony stood aside (an accurate description, whereas the cliché 'taking a back seat' would not be) while Hacker got to grips with immigration's concerns, the necessary papers and clearances that some staff lacked, the rates at which they were paid and the relations with suppliers. This did not compromise the discreet, almost clandestine, position he had sought at the New Yew when he agreed to Euphony's contract for the work was either within the restaurant itself or well away from the village. Euphony would have given the exercise as little attention as possible, cutting corners if she thought she could get away with it. Hacker understood that being seen to take it seriously was as important as doing so. Besides he had no desire that The Old Bell be put under a similar spotlight. It was not that he had anything to fear, far from it - for one thing he didn't employ any other staff except the occasional relief and his suppliers had never raised any problems. But he had moved to Birton Sodbury in the first place to avoid this sort of hassle, and while the Old Sods still kept a watching brief they had relaxed their vigilance from the early years. He had no desire to revive their interest, malevolent or otherwise, and knew how easy it was to be tarred by association.

15

While Hacker was resolving the New Yew crises, or trying to at any rate, Euphony was busy too. It had started with a phone call out of the blue from a major company based in London. Euphony had known of them since her brief stint as a trainee accountant, but had become increasingly aware in recent years as a result of their profile in the restaurant business. How could she not be when they were such dominant players in the market? They operated on both sides of the Atlantic and, in the words they used to investors, 'eschewed a Chairman and Chief Exec in favour of the American model of a President and Chief Operating Officer'. It was the latter who had rung her and at first she thought it was either a wind-up or some Machiavellian ruse the Old Sods might perpetrate. Her first reaction, therefore, was not to respond to the approach immediately but, claiming that it was not then convenient to speak, to ring Hedge Inc. herself. Despite their name, they weren't just in the business of buy-outs and maximising returns regardless, but had a long and enviable track record of running things.

Euphony realised that she might be over-reacting to what could be an innocent enquiry, but she was not prepared to take any risks. It might be paranoid, but she had some cause for caution. As long as she didn't take it to extremes, or let it dominate every interaction, being alert had its benefits. Taking the opportunity to show her sang-froid, Euphony did not ring back immediately but even after she had made a cup of tea found that only ten minutes had passed. She forced herself to wait another five before calling the number she had been given. She ought to have checked Directory Enquiries herself but it was too late for that. The phone only rang once before it was answered with "Hedge Inc. How can I help you?"

"Euphony Blurr here. A Mr Charles tried to ring me a few minutes ago. Is he free now?"

"I'm his PA. I'll put you through."

It took barely a moment before Euphony heard "Oh, hi there Euphony. Chuck Charles. Glad you can talk now."

Euphony found the mid-Atlantic twang re-assuring. She could imagine the Americans thought Chuck one of them while the British believed Mr Charles to be one of theirs. "That's OK," she said, "How can I help?"

"As you might expect we - Hedge Inc., that is - pride ourselves on knowing what's going on in the catering business, and we've been watching your operation for a while."

Euphony suspected this was flannel but it was the sort of balm she was prepared to put up with. On the other hand, she was nothing if not feisty and Hedge Inc. would have to make her an offer she couldn't refuse. "You surprise me. We've only being going a year, barely that."

"Look Euphony this is not something that I want to go into too much detail about on the phone. We admired the way you started up in a new place, but the resilience to come back a second time, especially given the situation, was even more impressive. And then to get the reviews you've got made us want to find out more."

"Thank you. But it's not for sale all the same."

Chuck Charles laughed. "That's not what we had in mind at all," he said.

"So what did you have in mind? This is hardly a social call to tell me of your admiration."

"Well, I don't want to say much more on the phone. Would it be possible to meet - at our expense, of course. We could send a driver to pick you up and meet either here in London or wherever you prefer."

Euphony was intrigued. Companies like Hedge Inc. didn't ring up without a serious purpose and Chuck Charles was clearly calling in his professional capacity, though she had no doubt that he would have had her personal past thoroughly investigated in any case.

"London will be fine," Euphony said. "But your driver can't come here. I'll get the train and he can meet me at the station there."

"OK, whatever you want. Go first-class. We'll be happy to pay."

"When were you thinking of?" she asked.

"What's today? Any time later this week will be fine. We'll move things around if we have to, but we wouldn't want to leave it too long."

"Friday will be fine," Euphony said. "How about 11.30 at your office?"

"That's ideal. It should only take a couple of hours and we'll lay on lunch. If you let my PA know what time your train gets in, we'll make sure someone is there to drive you in. Look forward to meeting you then."

"Fine. See you on Friday." Euphony rang off but not as quickly as Chuck Charles had. He clearly didn't hang about where business was concerned. Euphony wondered what he had in mind but no amount of guesswork could be more than just that. Rather than waste time and energy, she might as well wait to hear what he - they, she assumed - had to say. Going in with an open mind, and without expectations that might prove wide of the mark in any case, would be the best tactic and even, if it weren't, it was the only option available to her. Unless she decided to cancel, and there was certainly no reason for that.

16

Chuck Charles' PA showed Euphony into his office as soon as she arrived at Hedge Inc. It was a while since she had travelled first class but the morning had reminded her of the style that suited her. The comfort and ease of the train was magnified in the chauffeured car, and the smooth ride looked set to continue, at least for a while. Euphony was pleased to find that she was not to be the only woman in the room. Chuck Charles introduced her to the other three people sat at one end of the huge table in his office, all of whom were women, the company's Finance Director, Head of Marketing and Head of Sales - who also seemed to be keeping a note. Euphony sat down, next to the Finance Director in the other chair pulled out. Even with five of them in the room, most of the chairs were empty.

The Finance Director poured her some coffee.

"Euphony, let me welcome you to Hedge Inc. and explain why we invited you," Chuck Charles started. "But before I do, I just want to be sure that we can rely on your discretion. This conversation needs to be confidential to this room. I've asked Miranda to keep a record just so we're all clear. Normally, my PA would do this but she has to get some things off to America before they open for business."

"It depends what you want to discuss. I can't give you a blanket promise and I'm sure you wouldn't expect me to. Obviously, I'll decide on anything that affects the New Yew."

"I appreciate that. This doesn't concern the New Yew - at least not directly - nor the staff who work there. By the way we know about the staff problems and, as long as they're the sort of blip that every employer faces, they're totally irrelevant as far as we're concerned. No, this concerns our operation and as the information would be market sensitive, we need to be sure it will go no further."

"I don't have any problem with that then," said Euphony.

"The other thing I should say is that this is a preliminary discussion that commits neither you nor us to anything. If it works out, we can make it public in good time and in the way that suits us all. What we wouldn't want to happen is that our competitors get hold of it prematurely, or anybody draws the wrong conclusions. You know what journalists can do."

"That's fine. I'm keen to hear what you have to say."

"OK, I'll ask Miranda to start then."

The Head of Sales started by referring to the company's history of running restaurants throughout the UK, particularly in the south and west of England. The company pedigree was unquestioned and until the last year or so customer views had been almost universally positive. Despite the booming economy, however, there had been a noticeable downturn in the number of covers since then. The company was still making money but was no longer growing as it had been. The Finance Director added some figures to show that growth in the last two years was under 2% and falling. One way of recovering might be to open more restaurants, but if the concept was past its sell-by date this could bring even greater risk.

They didn't spell out what they meant by this but Euphony was quick to ask whether they thought they needed to take a step back to go forward again.

"That's just our assessment," said Chuck Charles. "We can make-over the menus without too much trouble but that's pointless if it's the concept itself that's stale. Doesn't matter how good the food, or how keenly priced, you've got to get people through the door first. The whole dining experience in other words."

"OK, so where do I fit in?" said Euphony, though she was beginning to get an idea.

"Lorrie, over to you," said Chuck Charles.

If the name didn't make it apparent that the Head of Marketing was American, her accent certainly did. "I'll come straight to the point. We've tried one or two ideas out in sample restaurants but either they turned people off or any initial interest quickly waned. So what we'd like to do is try out something based on your approach with the New Yew."

"Do you mean the décor or the food," Euphony paused, "or both?"

"As you can imagine, we don't want to replicate the New Yew nationwide. Our brand brings with it a lot of recognition and, as the figures show, a lot of loyalty. We owe it to our existing customers - and to our staff as well, come to that - to make this a gradual process. There's no call for a rush to ground zero. Anyway, we doubt there's a market for a New Yew makeover everywhere. What we were going to suggest, and I'm sure you'll understand our caution, is more in the nature of an experiment."

"You mean a trial?" Euphony asked.

"In essence, yes - but without the negative connotations, of course. A pilot is a more neutral way of thinking about it."

Chuck Charles broke in. "I can understand your apprehension, Euphony. We feel the same way ourselves. And, as I said at the start, this conversation is an exploration of the possibilities, an opening discussion, and it may get no further than that."

"Are you talking to anyone else?" Euphony asked.

"No, not yet."

"And you wouldn't have brought me here, if you didn't want to move forward on it."

"There's often a big gap between the ideal and the possible, though, so what we 'want' as you put it may turn out to be no more than a hope. It's certainly our aim, however. Let Lorrie explain."

"Euphony, what we had in mind," Lorrie continued, responding to Euphony's hesitance, "is to pick four restaurants. Ideally, they'll have some similarities in size and use, especially region, but there's no possibility that they will be totally comparable. One would stay as now, one would serve the New Yew menu for three months say, one would continue with the current menu but adopt the New Yew style and décor."

"And the fourth would get the full treatment?" Euphony asked, "house style and menu?"

"That's what we were thinking," Lorrie said. "Each would be its own before and after experiment, while offering some scope for comparison as well."

"What about the impact on the New Yew? If the full-blown mock-up does worst of all, where does that leave me?"

"There might be all sorts of explanations," said Chuck Charles. "Perhaps the location was wrong or the customers couldn't adapt or the appeal wasn't there for new ones. We might also re-brand it as, say, Edgeways - so there would be even less connection."

And little with Hedge Inc. either, Euphony thought.

"So, what's the point of trying it at all? You seem to have the explanations ready already."

"That's if it doesn't work," said Miranda. "Our leap of faith is that it will."

"And that's what we're asking of you too," said Chuck Charles. "We realise it must look like a huge risk but we'll certainly make it worth your while."

"I'll have to think about it," said Euphony

"We wouldn't expect anything else," he said. "But you do need to keep it to yourself for the moment."

Lorrie went to a flipchart standing in the corner of the room and turned over the front page to reveal the following diagram. "This might help."

		Impact		
Restaurant	**Planned change**	less	none	more
A	None			
B	Menu			
C	Style			
D	Both			

"Impact is probably receipts," Lorrie explained, "but it could be people in the short-term. Curiosity might bring customers through the door initially, but they might not spend any more. What we need in the longer term is an outcome for both - more customers and more spend. Though how we interpret the results depends on A, of course. If this continues to decline, then even those holding steady - those breaking even - would look good."

"I see," said Euphony. "And conversely, if A improves but the others do worse, the New Yew has had it."

"I can understand your position but that's not the way to think of it," said Chuck Charles. "Or only one way," he quickly added as he detected Euphony's mounting hostility. She disliked being patronised and Hedge Inc. needed to be careful not to antagonise her if they wanted her cooperation. "We'd make sure these restaurants were a long way from the New Yew. We wouldn't want your existing customers going there anyway. That would invalidate the results. But it also means that if things don't work out there should be no effect on the New Yew. You can carry on as before."

"There would be some impact on reputation," Euphony said.

"Perhaps," said Lorrie, "but just as likely not."

"That's easy for you to say," Euphony thought.

Chuck Charles turned to the Finance Director who had said little so far. "Pamela, why don't you tell Euphony what we had in mind?"

"OK. Obviously we would meet all the costs, including any travel or other expenses you incurred. First-class and five star throughout, needless to say. And we would pay you a retainer, subject to annual review, as well as a fee for the project."

"The retainer would be so we could continue the work after the initial project - if appropriate, though I'm sure it would be," said Chuck Charles. "We'd also pay a waiver, an indemnity if you like, against any downside."

"That sounds like you want to buy my silence as well as my help," said Euphony.

"We aim to cover all the bases. Think of it as a demonstration of our gratitude if - when - this makes a difference."

"Some might think it a bribe," Euphony thought to herself, though she didn't say so out loud. But she realised that this was how business was done, and Hedge Inc. had been around long enough to be able to discriminate between the barely legal and the definitely not. They made much of their ethical approach and had a Head of Ethics to manage their audit and social responsibilities. They took this as seriously as any other corporation and more so than many. There was no need to break the rules when often there was sufficient latitude to bend them. Possession might be nine-tenths of the law, but interpretation ran it a close second. The legal profession depended on it, and corporate lawyers were no different.

What Euphony did say was "That sounds like a lot of money?"

"I'm sure you'll understand that we don't want to go into the details at this stage," said Pamela, "but we're certainly thinking of six figures - plus all the expenses of course."

"You'll have to be a little clearer than that," Euphony said.

"We don't mind telling you that you wouldn't be far wrong if you had £200,000 in your head," said Chuck Charles. "That would be all three of course: the annual retainer, the fee and the waiver. In return, you'd have to sign a contract so that we're all clear what we're getting. If things get that far, that is."

"I'd need advice before signing any contract," Euphony said.

"Naturally. We wouldn't expect anything else."

"So how can I ask any questions and when would you want me to decide?" Euphony asked.

"Miranda, Lorrie and Pamela will be able to answer your questions. Ring my PA for their direct lines," he said. "In terms of hearing your decision, how does a fortnight from today sound?"

"Fine."

"But I need to emphasise that this is still a two-way process. We'll need to talk about it between ourselves too. So no guarantees," he said. "On the other hand, you may be able to tell how much thought Hedge Inc. have given this already. We don't make investments of any kind, cash or time and effort, if we don't plan to follow through if we can. Thanks for coming in."

The meeting was over and there had been no lunch. Euphony had much to think about on the journey back to Birton Sodbury and the New Yew.

17

Although Euphony was flattered that Hedge Inc. had approached her, she was unable to decide why they had. She had thought of asking Miranda, the Head of Sales, but as she was in a meeting when Euphony called had spoken to Lorrie instead.

"To be quite candid," Lorrie explained, "we did think first of some people who are better known, but decided that their profile might be a hindrance. If we'd gone for someone with name recognition, this might have been their project rather than our's. Also, the press could have interpreted it as a desperate rescue mission. Nor would it have been easy to make it fit with our brand."

Euphony had enough experience to know that those who claimed candour rarely were. Often it was designed to conceal rather than enlighten. On the other hand Lorrie had said more than she needed to.

"But there must be many others who would jump at the chance to work with Hedge Inc. on their mid-market concept?" Euphony asked, realising as she did so that she was weakening her own position.

"That's right. We just hope you're among them."

"So you're still keen to proceed?" Euphony asked. Her worst fear was that she would agree only to find the offer withdrawn. At first she had been tempted to decline but what did she have to lose really? Time certainly, and less attention on the New Yew itself, but on the other hand this was an opportunity that was unlikely to come again and even if it didn't work out she would have the money to expand her own business.

"We haven't changed our mind, if that's what you mean," Lorrie said.

"How long do you expect it would take?"

"We thought a year to test out the impact fully and iron out any seasonal variations."

"That's your project timescale, surely? I was thinking of how much time you'd want me for."

"I'm not sure I know the answer to that. As long as it takes to work with the architects and fitters to re-design the third and fourth restaurants and work with the staff for the two that are changing their menus. No more than three months overall probably including some refresher training."

"Chuck Charles said something about only running the menu for three months."

Lorrie laughed. "That's why he's Chief Operating Officer. Fortunately there are operations experts as well who don't let their optimism outrun their experience. It will need to be longer than that, though we will have a good idea after three months. For the restaurants that are altered it will be a year unless the results are obvious before then."

"OK, I'll think about it and get back to you."

"If you have any more questions, don't hesitate to ring again. Or even ring one of the others and see what their take is on these questions."

"Thanks," said Euphony. "I appreciate that but it probably won't be necessary."

Euphony knew she should get some advice elsewhere, even ask Hacker what he thought, but she was more certain that she wasn't going to. It was not just about being stubborn and independent, it was also about being prepared to back her instincts. There wasn't much of a risk in any case and certainly not enough to put off a calculated gambler like Euphony. She would require some impartial assessment of the contract and, though Hacker's caution and attention to detail would have been ideal, this would not be appropriate. It would have to be a lawyer with business and employment experience. Perhaps Hacker would be able to suggest someone and perhaps Hedge Inc. would consider it one of her expenses.

He couldn't but they would.

18

Many of the newspaper headlines mimicked the Hedge Inc. press release without further investigation. 'Gets Blurr Makeover' and 'Hedge Blurred' were two examples. The *Financial Times* thought the initiative might represent deeper problems in the business and, in a rare attempt at a joke, asked 'Hedge to come out the other side?' 'Hedge Inc. in bed with Blurr' was a gossip column heading that speculated as to the company's reason for choosing Euphony as their partner. It might have set other hares running but at the time there was little interest in pursuing any salacious aspects of the story.

Euphony had expected more probing from the press but either their attention was elsewhere or, with the demise of investigative journalism, things had to land in their laps or involve somebody already known to them for their interest to be aroused. This was more probable if the person was someone they had previously built up as a celebrity and could now demolish, or someone they thought due a come-uppance. Breaking reputations must have felt particularly rewarding if you had first made them. Those the press labelled "icons" had to be handled more carefully, with their demise tackled in stages so as not to alarm readers unduly; but this had the same advantage as any long-running saga, like a soap opera, of adding followers. If Euphony's view was cynical, her experiences told her that this was the safest approach. She was certainly fortunate that neither 24-hour news nor social media were yet widespread. This would multiply the sources, many of which had even less regard for the facts than a press release, as well as increasing the demand for them to fill the time available.

This muted public reaction was accompanied by a wide range of responses from the restaurant staff themselves. A few were positive, particularly where it was only the menu that would change, but most were apprehensive about a change in style that would move them away from the Hedge brand they were used to and with which they felt comfortable. In the restaurant where both the menu and style would change, all the staff were tense and some were understandably anxious for their futures. Not generally noted for her sensitivity to the views of others, Euphony was alive to their concerns in this instance and prepared to put in whatever it took to win them over to the New Yew style. It helped that it was not her money that was on the line and indeed this was what Hedge Inc. were paying her for. She was prepared to go softly, at least for a while, but her patience was not endless and Hedge Inc. would be expecting her to drive through the changes if that turned out to be required. The staff might delay, and Euphony would attempt to allay their concerns, but they were not in any position to prevent the initiative proceeding. Nor did they have behind them a Union to protect their interests if these were forgotten or overlooked. Nevertheless, Euphony sought to win their acquiescence if not their approval, for their endorsement would be critical to success. They found it flattering too that staff from Hedge Inc. were showing an interest in them and not just in the bottom line, their usual focus. Even Chuck Charles paid a visit before the restaurant re-launched.

Euphony had been conscious of the Hedge Inc. spotlight throughout the process, but she was also aware, as were the local staff, that their attention could be terminated as rapidly as it had been generated. Hedge Inc. had not survived for so long without being ruthless when they judged circumstances demanded it and this would be no exception if it did not deliver the results they sought. The pressure for Euphony was on her reputation, but for the staff it was their jobs that were at stake. They had to make it work. And they did.

Chuck Charles and the Hedge Inc. Directors were delighted as growth recovered at the made-over restaurants and the company share price stabilised. Euphony was almost as relieved as the staff. It appeared that they had pulled it round though only time would tell whether they had also pulled it off.

19

Euphony's relationship with Hedge Inc. had been solely a business one to this point but, if Chuck Charles had not provided lunch at their first meeting, he made up for it with a dinner to celebrate her success. The combination of euphoria and alcohol relaxed both their inhibitions, and relief soon became passion. "I've misused my body for so long," Euphony said to him, "it's about time someone else had a go." He might usually seek to separate business and pleasure, preferring to act the single-minded businessman or at least to be thought a gentleman, but few could resist such an invitation and Chuck Charles was not about to forgo the opportunity.

Euphony had no expectations the following day that this would prove any more than yet another one-night stand, an experience she had been through many times over the years. Chuck Charles must have felt the same for he had left before Euphony woke up. But when he texted her later that day and suggested they meet again, she began to view things differently.

Euphony's makeover had been so successful that Chuck Charles could now promote this as the house style to the board of Hedge Inc. He had been ready to advocate hard if need be but they took little persuading. It came as no surprise when Euphony was commissioned to roll this out to all their restaurants. Euphony's retainer was to be replaced by royalties as each new restaurant came on-stream, thus maintaining her interest in seeing the programme through. She could no longer be hands-on but would remain in overall charge, overseeing the initiative and providing the vision. Her job would be to train the trainers, many of whom treated her as a guru or oracle. There was some polite opposition from the company's bankers, and many local managers had concerns, but while both groups could protest they were powerless to do more in the face of the company's determination and the Board decision. If they didn't like it, there would be others who did, a powerful incentive to express their concerns decorously. It was always clear that the juggernaut would win. And neither group was prepared to stand in its path.

This was not a good moment for either Euphony or Chuck Charles to become confused about their motives, to replace purpose with passion or mistake emotion for logic. But if an overpowering sense of relief had provided their bond initially, they were powerless to resist the lust that now took them over. Euphony had an office in the Hedge Inc. building and nobody was surprised that they spent so much time in each other's company. "You can't have too much of a good thing" their motto - as Shakespeare almost, but not quite, put it in *As You Like It*.

But the restaurants were not prospering as vigorously as had their relationship. At first things appeared to have gone well, but business tailed off even before the make-over programme was completed. It was now Chuck Charles whose job was on the line, and forced to give more attention to the business, he had correspondingly less time to devote to Euphony. Inevitably, their relationship cooled. Euphony was not overly concerned about this; they were both adults, neither had been hurt and it might still be possible to find the odd spark among the smouldering embers if the occasion arose.

It was different for Hedge Inc. The company was not forced into liquidation, but there were times when administration seemed the most likely option. Eventually, this was avoided by some radical pruning that saw the firm half its previous size. The New Yew re-branding was put aside and the company did its best to erase the episode from its history.

It was not so straightforward for the staff, some of whom had stood by Hedge Inc. for many years as its fortunes fluctuated, but now found themselves expendable. The company was in the recovery ward but there was no such rehabilitation for the cooks and waiting staff laid off with very little notice and less severance pay. In some parts of the country there was no equivalent employment and they had to fall back on whatever minimum wage jobs they could find. Others were so demoralised by the experience that nobody would hire them. A few did get jobs with competitors.

Euphony was particularly sorry for those who had embraced the make-over enthusiastically and become its advocates and trainers within Hedge Inc. They were not only made redundant like many of their colleagues but had the added burden of blame. In some cases they lost their friends as well as their job and home. A few had been the glue that held their restaurant team together and they had lost everything. Not all were young enough to start again.

Chuck Charles had a just sufficient track record from the past to hold on to his post, perhaps in part because the Board could not find an obvious replacement given the extent to which the company was smaller than before. They had tried, but had not been able to convince any possible successors that smaller meant leaner. The people they approached recognised that the losses might have been staunched but were not convinced that the wounds would heal in any timeframe compatible with their career plans. The Board had to content themselves with clawing back some of the bonuses they had previously awarded Chuck Charles. As these were mainly in the form of shares, and the price had plunged with the company's prospects, he made a huge loss on paper but very little in reality. Older investors who had relied on the modest dividends to boost their income in retirement were not so fortunate.

The company was delighted that Euphony was prepared to walk away from her contract without insisting that they paid her off. This was arguably the most honourable thing she had done, though it had the unspoken but added benefit that the gossip columns were less likely to salivate over something in the past. Exposing the personal makeover that she and Chuck Charles engaged in would have been of interest to readers when they and Hedge Inc. were at the top of their game. Much less so once they and it were yesterday's news.

Hacker had kept the New Yew itself ticking over, despite the best efforts of the Old Sods, so she at least had somewhere to move on to. She was not downhearted by Hedge Inc.'s demise, having been through much worse in the past and finding succour in a philosophical view of life. Some might have thought the absence of remorse or even regret psychopathic, but Euphony knew better. After all wasn't too shit simply the past participle of touché? Something else was always around the corner.

And so it proved.

20

Hacker was able to hand the New Yew back to Euphony in better shape than she'd left it. Even the Old Sods seemed to have been pacified, though it was always possible that their recent restraint just meant that they were stoking themselves up for the next onslaught. As Hacker understood it, Euphony was returning on a full-time basis so he was delighted to have his attention restricted to The Old Bell once more. He wasn't on holiday but no longer having to split his time between the pub and the restaurant made it feel like it. It was as if he had taken off his formal outfit in favour of something more comfortable.

Euphony fully intended to devote her time completely to the New Yew but it did not take her long to find out that there was little for her to do. The staff all knew what was required of them and were determined to show her that, though they might miss Hacker, they were able to deliver in his absence. Euphony toyed with some marginal changes but it was clear that neither the staff nor the regular diners saw any need for them. So smoothly was the operation running that any tinkering might have disrupted it. Euphony was reduced to checking the accounts, never her forté.

"What do you think I should do?" she asked Hacker.

"If I was you, I'd take the opportunity to catch your breath. Things won't always be this smooth and no doubt you still have some things to process from the Hedge Inc. debacle."

But Euphony didn't see it like that. The past was just that and it could have been much worse. Furthermore, her bank balance had never been so healthy, better even than before she had bought Riddler's Yard.

This might provide some people with a cushion, even a refuge if things turned sour, but for Euphony it was an opportunity. The question was an opportunity for what?

It hadn't been the New Yew cuisine, or even the change of style, that had brought Hedge Inc. to its knees, but the speed with which it had been pushed through. The staff had done their best to keep up, indeed the training had fortified them, but the existing customers were left floundering and there were too few new ones to close the gap. A gentler pace of change was required.

Euphony went away for a long weekend to consider her options. Staying in top-end hotels had been necessary for the Hedge Inc. task but she had never been a fan of them. She had checked into a smaller, more bijou operation that some would have described as boutique but traded under the banner of 'country house accommodation'. Euphony began to consider the possibilities of combining this with the New Yew cuisine. The initial outlay would be substantial, but not as huge as mass market or other mainstream possibilities. If she started small she could manage it on her own and not require the backers, financial or otherwise, that larger operations would require.

In the absence of anywhere else obvious to begin, she had asked her hosts what they thought of it. Though not interested personally, they thought her idea worth pursuing and, more to the point, were aware of a couple of people who were trying to sell up - not because they couldn't make their operations pay but simply because they had decided to retire. If accurate, these were leads worth following up. Armed with the details, and having asked that they not be alerted in advance, Euphony went off to see for herself.

The first of these was more like a country club, with its own golf course, swimming pool and health spa. It attracted locals to these facilities at off-peak times as well as catering for those who wanted to stay. Euphony decided it was out of her range and never even broached the possibilities with the owners.

The second, however, was entirely dependent on people who had been attracted to the surrounding countryside and chose to stay there because of the reputation the owners had developed over thirty years. Euphony found this much more promising, even more so when it transpired that the owners had already built a home for their retirement nearby and wanted to settle into it full-time as soon as possible. The staff had been with them a long time and the current owners were keen that their interests be secured along with any sale. This had put off prospective purchasers in the past but made it even more attractive to Euphony. The price sought was just about affordable and, if she had to borrow some additional capital initially, the assets were sufficient and the occupancy rate high enough to make this a risk worth taking.

Euphony made a half-hearted attempt to haggle over the price, more as a matter of form than with any expectation that the owners would reduce it further than they already had. Euphony was not surprised that they wouldn't and accepted their valuation as gracefully as she could. All the practical details were swiftly settled and within a couple of months Euphony was the owner. At twelve beds there was some scope to increase occupancy, perhaps through cut-price mid-week packages, but an alternative strategy would be to move up-market and charge more. While the addition of New Yew cuisine made this feasible, she had no desire to alienate her existing customers before she had replaced them with new ones. This made no business sense and if she had learned anything from the Hedge Inc. experience it was not to rush things; far better to let them evolve gradually so that there was a sustainable basis on which to build. This had the additional merit of not spooking the staff, and extra mid-week packages would not interfere with the existing clientele. They would have to accept the New Yew menu, of course, whereas new customers would not know any different, but this could be adjusted in the short-term if necessary.

The other thing she had learned was not to put your own money on the line if others were prepared to risk their's. Some might think this a questionable stance, even an amoral one, but Hedge Inc. had also confirmed for Euphony that there was no place for sentiment in business. There was no way the two could be mixed successfully, not at any rate if your yardstick was profit and the latter was the only way to keep people in work. The justification might be tortuous but at least there was one.

Consequently, as the mix of country house accommodation and New Yew started to take off, Euphony decided against expanding the business herself. Rather she invited some bankers to try it themselves with the intention that, if they liked it, they would help promote the approach as a franchise which others could buy into. She sold it to them as the Third Way, a strapline that was both brief and illuminating. Some said it was just the investment opportunity they had been waiting for. Euphony doubted this but if it helped them sleep more easily she was happy to go along with it. She soon had the financial backing she sought.

The first step was to start a new company and prepare the necessary materials to send out to prospective franchisees. Although it was called Third Way, the PR firm misheard, putting together a package for the HerdWay brand. By the time Euphony saw the proofs, 'HerdWay' appeared in nearly every line. It would not have been impossible to change it but it was more than just replacing this with 'Third Way'. Unbelievably, the two extra spaces in the latter meant that from the second page on everything was out of synch. Internal page references, and as in any business document there were many of these, were wrong; items that should have been on the same page were now separated in ways that made the documents look unprofessional. The PR company were contrite but made it clear that they expected Euphony to pay for the changes. For her part she decided to accept that there was at least a rural connection to HerdWay, not a strong one perhaps but enough to make the case if it proved necessary. Critically, 'Third Way' could remain the public face; only the franchisees need be aware of the 'HerdWay' connection.

21

As if this was not a bad enough start, the first batch of prospective franchisees included the Cowards from Birton Sodbury.

"Any idea why?" Euphony asked Hacker.

"They have got a very attractive home and it's definitely a country house. Though I'm very surprised that they'd open it up to other people. One of the things Cecilia is known for is the select few who get over her threshold."

"Perhaps they need to supplement their income then?"

"Or, which is much more likely, perhaps she's up to something else. On the other hand ...", Hacker replied.

"You surely don't think I should consider them?"

"Good God, no. What I was going to say was that some might prefer her on the inside."

"As someone who knows her and what the Old Sods are capable of, would you advise me to take that line?"

"No, I wouldn't. They're hardly the ideal hosts and even if she upped her game I'd always suspect her motives," Hacker said. "But perhaps she doesn't expect to be taken on. Indeed, she may be hoping you turn her down flat so that she has a grievance to gripe about."

"So, what's the way out of that?"

"You could always go through the motions of vetting the proposal and turn her down for lack of experience or on a technicality. Alternatively, you could call her bluff so that she's forced to withdraw."

"That sounds risky. She might not withdraw and, even if she did, it could take a lot more time than I have – and certainly more than I'd want to spend on her machinations."

"What I think would be a tactical error would be for you to get involved yourself. That may be what she's hoping for, entangling you in a grievance that would get in the way of anything else."

"I wish I understood what I'd done to incur her hatred."

"You don't have to do anything. Indeed, you haven't done. Simply suggesting change would be enough to set her off." Hacker paused. "Do you know anyone that you could ask to do the vetting for you? They'd need sufficient standing in the industry to put them beyond her challenge."

"I'll give it some thought. You're right though, I need to keep this at arm's length."

Apart from dealing with the Cowards, an issue that Euphony handed on to a carefully briefed and experienced colleague hired for the purpose, the other initial applications from franchisees were clearly bona fide and went without a hitch. A few months later the first half dozen Third Way, or should it be HerdWay, operations were up and running. Euphony had forgotten her intention to take it more slowly than had been possible with Hedge Inc., her enthusiasm and impatience getting the better of her. But, unlike the positive press that the New Yew had gathered when it started, a not insignificant factor in persuading Hedge Inc. to approach her, the reviewers were not enthusiastic about the Third Way. The general opinion seemed to be that it was neither one thing nor the other, a hotch-potch, traducing both the country house and New Yew traditions. They might have been even more caustic had they known about the HerdWay brand.

Fortunately, though, the customers appeared less concerned with the niceties that worried the reviewers. It was different, but with features they were comfortable with, and perhaps most importantly they didn't feel they were being taken for a ride. The hotels were giving them value for money and at the end of the day that was more important than what the glossy magazines thought. Occupancy rates started to climb, the existing franchisees were delighted, more were applying every day, and Euphony was soon making money hand over fist. Even the Coward cloud wouldn't last forever.

Jeremiah Coolcat, the independent assessor of the Coward application, reported in detail and on time, recommending their rejection. Not only had Euphony made sure it was a 'he' as Cecilia might find it harder to bully a man she was not married to, the man chosen had a reputation as forbidding as his name. Not only were there the expected difficulties due to the Cowards' limited experience and motivation, the capital requirements to open a private home to the public, concerns over their age and ability, but Coolcat had gone so far as to garner the views of their neighbours – not only the implications of more people and traffic but on the Cowards themselves. They had provided glowing references from the Bogeys and positive ones from other Old Sods, but even so Euphony suspected they must have called in some debts to obtain them. Coolcat's assessment was sceptical that these genuinely reflected their character, let alone their abilities, and in any case did not find them an adequate counter to the rest of his report. This was damning.

So pleased was Euphony that she thought about contacting the Cowards herself to pass on the conclusion. Hacker argued against it and ultimately his was the view that prevailed. Better for Euphony to keep out of direct contact so that there was no confusion in the Coward minds and so that Euphony should not be seen to gloat. It was the outcome that mattered and not being present at the dénouement should not detract from her enjoyment of it. If only it took the wind out of Cecilia's sails rather than spurring her on to other attempts at sabotage. The owners of country houses after all were, if not her natural milieu, certainly the sort of people with whom she identified. The question was whether they were more interested in running a profitable business or undermining it.

22

While Hacker enjoyed making things happen, he had reached a point in his life where he was no longer ambitious for himself and, if truth be told, there were advantages in being a bystander. He admired Euphony's resilience, for her antidote to failure was to plunge in to the next adventure in the expectation that it would be a success. His approach was different, preferring to retreat and, if not exactly lick his wounds, recover in his own time by processing the disappointments. He wasn't close enough to Euphony to know whether she did this too when nobody was looking, but somehow he doubted it. The casual observer might contrast his thoughtful and introspective approach with her more active one. She was certainly more determined than he, but it was not just that she was more extravert. That was the sort of psychological judgement that categorised but did not explain. 'Banging on regardless as if nothing else mattered' might be how the layman would put it and, while this was nearer the mark in Hacker's view, still didn't nail it entirely. Part of him was in awe, speechless - but in shock as much as in admiration. There must be a clinical term for such a condition but it was more than just her being hyperactive. Try as he might he couldn't quite put his finger on it.

What had started as anxiety and then had turned to concern was now a worry. Hacker might have been even more alarmed had he known that Third Way was really HerdWay. But it was prospering and so was Euphony. Unfortunately, it was not only her bank balance that was swelling. She had been encouraged to undertake leadership seminars, the outcome of which was slightly preferable to 'get rich quick' ones in that the audience got something out of them, not just the speaker. Euphony enjoyed them, reminding her of past successes training the staff of the New Yew and Hedge Inc. and more recently alongside the franchisees. As for most people, if you enjoy something it is more likely to be repeated and even become your raison d'etre. This was the case for Euphony, but the risk for her, as for everybody, was of coming to the wrong conclusions about strengths. Euphony's enthusiasm shone through her presentations and because she had experiences, ups and downs, that audiences could relate to, she was much in demand. While such infectious enthusiasm would have carried her far, as it has many others, it depended for its impact on its relationship to the content of her talks. Euphony could talk successfully about leadership in the hospitality business and the catering trade, and there were some universal truths, that enabled her to extend it to leadership in general. Her assessment, though, was that it was her that the audience came to hear and that her message ought to be one about life, what she had learned from it and how everybody else could benefit from her example.

Hacker soon moved on from worry to despair as Euphony's messianic delusions became increasingly obvious. She had taken up lay preaching and talked about buying out what was left of Hedge Inc. Hacker's attempts to reason with her were of no avail and trying to dissuade her from the Hedge Inc. purchase was met with defiance. For his sanity and peace of mind he brought an end to the New Yew contract, content just to run The Old Bell. In order to take his mind off Euphony and stretch himself, he decided to bring it up to date and re-name it 'The Old Bull'. Birton Sodbury was still semi-rural and this might make it more so. He would have called it 'A Load of Bullocks', but knew the Old Sods would never let him get away with it.